THE NEFARIOUS NEMESIS AND THE WEDDING JINX

A POINT MUSE COZY PARANORMAL MYSTERY
BOOK 8

KELLY ETHAN

 Created with Vellum

A shout out to all those that have helped me with this series.
You rock!!

THE NEFARIOUS NEMESIS AND THE WEDDING JINX

A POINT MUSE COZY PARANORMAL MYSTERY BOOK 8

There's a furious damsel in a wedding dress, a killer stalking the Harrow clan, and a nosy Librarian turned sleuth. Let the mayhem begin…

Just one day. That's all Xandie Meyers, aka the Librarian to the Supernatural Great Library of Alexandria, wanted. One calm, mayhem free day to get married. But this is Point Muse, and nothing ever goes to plan.

It's wedding planner versus Elspeth Harrow in a fight to the altar. But accidents keep happening to derail the wedding and multiple bodies turn up. Just how far will her grandmother go? Because Elspeth has a policy. Whatever happens, the last Harrow standing wins. And Elspeth never loses, even if she has to cheat.

Unfortunately, the matriarch of the Harrow clan has too many secrets and some of them are about to come to light…

Like who is that mysterious, amber-eyed man lurking around town? And what is his connection to Elspeth Harrow? Xandie has no choice but to swing into Sherlock Librarian mode and investigate.

Suddenly it's not about the tragic, puffy, bridesmaids' dresses, but who will survive the day...

If you like snarky dialogue, murder, and mayhem, then you'll love the last installment in Kelly Ethan's Point Muse Mysteries, a cozy paranormal mystery series.

<u>Unlock the mayhem of The Nefarious Nemesis and the Wedding Jinx!</u>

ONE

"You're a dead Harrow walking."

Alexandra Meyers, a.k.a. Xandie, Librarian to the Supernatural Great Library of Alexandria, lifted her head from the table and glared at her younger cousin, Holly Harrow. "Meyers. Not Harrow."

"Pfft." Holly waved a hand in the air. "Last name doesn't matter. You're a Harrow, and Elspeth will stalk you into the nuthouse...or until you reinstate her as your wedding planner."

"Geez. You fired her?" Lila, another cousin, placed a platter of chocolate orange *pick-me-up* cakes on the table. "You're brave, or stupid, or both. It could go either way." Lila shoved the baked goods at her cousin. "Gorge away. You need the energy boost more than we do."

Xandie grabbed a cake and took a large bite, waiting for the tingly hit of Lila's witchy gifts. As a baker, every ounce of Lila's Harrow witchiness poured into her baking. Need a confidence boost? Head to Heart's Delight Bakery and order the lemon *you-can-do-it* cupcake. Need a more mellow hit for those of the hyperactive bent? Munch on

Lila's marsh-*mellow-out* slice. Just don't eat at the bakery when Lila has a bad day. Xandie shuddered internally at the memory of the rotten food fight that erupted after Lila's gift had gone haywire. Right now, Xandie needed any kind of boost she could get. "Elspeth's drunk on planning power. She wanted me to make my entrance on a vampire elephant. She thought the red flaming eyes made a nice contrast to my pastel color scheme." Grabbing another cake, she chewed in a determined fashion, glaring at her cousins.

"Hey." Holly held up a hand. "I voted no. Those vampire-infected animals shed way too many germs." She shuddered, then checked her temperature with the back of her hand.

Holly, the quiet planner of the trio, had a preoccupation with germs. A half banshee, she worked at the Elysian Fields Funeral Home and had amber colored eyes. In fact, all three cousins sported amber eyes and varying shades of brown hair. In Holly's case, her smooth hair hung in a short chin-length bob with a blunt fringe. Lila's lay in a tangled curly brown mess down her back, and Xandie's shoulder length hair tended to frizz. "The blood-raging elephant was the last straw. I snapped. It wasn't my fault. She drove me to it." She thumped the table.

Lila patted Xandie's clenched fist. "We know, sweetie. But it doesn't mean you aren't on Elspeth's hit list. She'll hound you until she gets what she wants."

"Zach's already hired a local wedding planner," Xandie added and picked at a discoloration on the white-colored table. "She apparently has no issues with bringing the wedding in on time. I can't believe Elspeth sent all the invitations out. We hadn't even decided on a date yet. Now she's sent them out magically, and we have to hurry up and plan the wedding or risk offending everyone. Half the people we don't even have contact details for. Blasted magic." Xandie dropped her head onto the tabletop and mumbled something into the wood.

"Can you translate your crazed mumblings?" Lila rapped knuckles on the back of her cousin's head.

Xandie turned her head to the side. "Maybe we should elope. Get the deed done in peace and quiet."

Holly snorted and wandered over to the bakery's front window. "Then everyone will be after you, instead of just Elspeth."

"I wonder how Zach feels about moving to Antarctica?" Her fiancé wanted whatever made Xandie happy. His side of the family were mainly bear shifters. As long as she supplied honey-based products at regular intervals during the reception, they were happy. It was the Harrow side she had to worry about.

"Uh, Xandie?" Holly peered out through the window and along Main Street.

"If Elspeth's marching along Main Street, tell me now so I can do a runner. Otherwise, I don't want to know."

"Did you bring Theo into town this morning, or is he back at the Library?"

Frowning, Xandie tapped her short, buffed nails on the tabletop. "He wanted to come for a ride, so I brought him and Horatio down on my bike. I think they're in the kitchen. Why?"

Holly tapped the window. "I think you need to see this for yourself." The faint brassy tone of a trumpet drifted in from the street.

Lila and Xandie cleared their seats in record time as they bolted to the window. Noses pressed against the glass, they tried to make out what was happening.

"Why is everyone standing around outside?" If this was

an Elspeth protest parade, Xandie would take the high ground and ignore it. Zach was right, the power had gone to Elspeth's head. Someone needed to stand strong against her for the good of their wedding.

"No festivals organized as far as I know." Holly fell silent for a few seconds. "I think I recognize the music." She left the window and opened the bakery door wide.

The bright tunes of a trumpet clashed with the mellow tones of a French horn.

Lila and Xandie followed Holly out onto the sidewalk.

Xandie pushed past an older man with a brassy redhead next to him, watching the spectacle unfold. "What has she done now?"

The redhead slipped in next to Xandie and clapped her hands. "I love a good parade."

"Not this kind of one," Lila mumbled as she crowded in behind.

"Hecate's cursed loins. Tell me she didn't," Xandie screeched.

"Oh, she did." Holly pointed at the knee-high procession of ceramic gnomes marching down Main Street, with a brass band playing Chopin's funeral march.

Lila hooted. "See the little guy at the front? She's given him a furry back to his wedding suit. A ceramic bear shifter in a tux."

"And look at the little gnome in the wedding dress. Her brown hair is teased out as far as it can go. Looks like she's wearing a brown pumpkin on her head." The redhead jiggled up and down and clapped her hands. "This town is darling."

"It's certainly something and not a surprise to anyone living in Point Muse."

Something in the older man's tone caught Xandie's

attention. He sounded familiar with Point Muse and its penchant for mayhem. But she'd never seen him in town before. He stood a little taller than Xandie's five foot five and sported a receding grey puffy haircut that had been sprayed to within an inch of its hairy life. His dapper suit looked a little threadbare at the elbows and something familiar about him nagged at her...

The older man turned and stared at Xandie, tipping his chin in acknowledgement before he shuffled his redheaded partner farther down the street.

Xandie stared open mouthed at the elderly man's retreating back.

"There's a parade of cursed ceramic gnomes in wedding attire meant to imitate you and your bear shifter, police chief beloved marching along to a funeral dirge, and you're staring at some random guy?" Lila stepped up to Xandie and peered down the street as well. "What's up with that? Is he an escaped killer out for blood?"

"Worse. I think."

Bracing herself against Holly, Lila nodded. "Lay it on me, cuz."

"He's the guy I saw Elspeth talking to on the docks below the Library a little while ago. Remember when that fae, Lady Rose, said something bad was coming? Harrow on Harrow?" Xandie pointed dramatically down Main Street. "That old guy has amber eyes."

Holly shoved Lila away from her. "It's not possible. Harrows only have girls. Hecate knows when the last male was born to the Harrow line. They're mythical in our family."

"Or Elspeth knows," Xandie muttered darkly.

"And right now, it's a nasty prank war between the two of you until you give in and reappoint her as your wedding planner. You won't get a straight answer out of her until you give her what she wants," Lila pointed out. "Maybe the old guy likes colored contacts?"

"Just because he has amber eyes doesn't mean he's an elusive male Harrow." Holly pursed her lips. "But it is like Elspeth to hide such a big mystery. It's not like she's an open book about her past."

Elspeth's past was scattered with misdeeds, black ops, and mayhem. The wicked witch never divulged a secret unless it benefited her, and the amber-eyed man was a definite secret. Xandie rubbed her forehead, an Elspeth-induced headache beginning to brew. "And the secret meeting between the two of them and the warning from the fae lady?"

Lila wrapped an arm around Xandie and drew her cousin back inside the bakery. "I think you need to eat more of my *pick-me-up* cakes and focus on your Elspeth wedding issue."

Xandie slumped into a chair. Her cousins meant well, but she had a horrid feeling that Mr. Amber Eyes and Elspeth were on a collision course, and her wedding was the battleground. People crowded the counter of the bakery, distracting her from her woes for a moment. Almost every table in the room was occupied. At least Elspeth's cursed ceramic gnome wedding procession had been good for business. Xandie's gaze drifted over the bakery's patrons before snagging on a muscled man in his twenties with a short brown buzz cut. He toyed with his coffee and stared out the window, not making eye contact with anyone. The guy had the right idea. She was done with socializing. All Xandie wanted to do was get back to her normal, sane, supernatural Library.

"Gird your loins, we have incoming," Holly intoned.

The bakery door swung open, and Elspeth Harrow, matriarch of the Harrow family and wicked witch extraordinaire, paused in the doorway. She spotted Xandie and her cousins and sauntered over with a smirk. Her talking, mouthy, ever-hungry pug minion, Colin, pranced on her heels. "Well, well. If it isn't the great betrayer."

Xandie pointed at her grandmother. "Don't push me, Elspeth Harrow. I have a headache."

Elspeth placed a hand dramatically over her emerald green, velour-covered, bony chest. "Woe is me. My treacherous granddaughter has a headache. The sky is falling. What shall Point Muse do? Maybe you need to ban your beloved grandmother from planning her first granddaughter's wedding before she dies of old age. Wait." Elspeth pointed a finger at Xandie. "You've already done that."

Xandie dropped her head back on the chair, staring at the bakery ceiling. That old adage that you couldn't pick your family was so true. Who on earth would pick a wig-wearing, jogging-suit-loving, wicked witch as the head of the family? Sighing, Xandie sat up and looked at Elspeth. "You wanted blood-hungry elephants at my wedding. That was the last straw. Simple. That's all we wanted."

Elspeth pretended to spit on the floor. "Simple is overrated. Impact, pizzazz. That's what's needed at a witch wedding."

"You sent the invitations out without checking with us. We hadn't even set an actual date. Now the invitations have gone out magically, and they can't be recalled. We can't even reach half the wedding guests to change the date. We have to rush the planning or risk offending magically gifted guests and starting a blood feud," Xandie growled. "You could have asked."

Elspeth flipped a long green wig curl over a shoulder. "Anyone would think you didn't want to get married."

"Argh," Xandie screeched and launched herself at her grandmother with hands outstretched.

Holly snagged her cousin around the waist and drew her closer to the counter where Lila's brownie employee, Hester, observed with a smirk.

"Don't do it. You'll regret it. We still haven't found the resting place of the last person who tried to strangle Elspeth," Holly whispered.

"Maybe she's hangry. I get that a lot." Colin, Elspeth's pug minion, wandered over to the kitchen door and narrowly avoided Lila as she swung through, slamming it shut hard behind her.

"We have a problem," Lila said.

Xandie sagged against Holly and blew out a breath. *Point Muse, the center for all things chaotic. When isn't there a problem?* "I'm fine now." She pushed Holly's hands away and straightened, resolutely ignoring her grandmother. "What's the issue?"

Lila's face paled. "Theo and Horatio." She raised a trembling hand toward the kitchen before stuttering to a stop.

Come to think of it, her black cat guardian to the Library had been exceptionally quiet in the kitchen for a karaoke-loving feline. Xandie spun and glared at Elspeth. "What have you done?"

Elspeth beamed a smug smile at her granddaughter. "Nothing but revel in the chaos and mayhem that planning a wedding causes." She dropped the smile. "Oh, wait. You fired me. No. More. Planning." She bellowed the last word, and the patrons in the bakery ducked under the tables. Everyone except the man still staring out the window.

Elspeth crossed her arms over her chest. "Besides, why do you always blame me?"

"Because it's always Elspeth-related." Xandie bolted to the kitchen door and froze in the doorway as she took in the scene.

Her grumpy black cat, Theo, a.k.a. Theophilus, ancient Greek guardian to the Supernatural Great Library of Alexandria, along with his pet imp, Horatio, were trussed up on the kitchen counter, next to a sink full of steaming hot water. Little grey hairless bodies danced around the trussed-up duo, waving their hands, and screeching in high-pitched tones every few seconds.

Lila, Holly, and Elspeth crowded behind Xandie and accidentally pushed her into the room.

Theo whipped his head around and glared at the Librarian. "I blame you and your bridezilla obsession with your wedding. Would it have killed you to let the old hag plan the festivities?"

Opening and closing her mouth a few times, Xandie turned and stared wide-eyed at her grandmother.

"Hey. For once, I didn't mastermind this torture session. Those imps are attracted by chaos and mayhem and the possibility of violence. This wasn't me." Elspeth peered at Theo. "Hang on, is he wearing a miniature apron?"

Everyone in the kitchen leaned forward, staring.

"Don't look at me. I'm hideous," Theo wailed as a large bunch of imps tried to throw a rope over the faucet and attach the other end of it to the cat and his pet.

"I love dogs? You're wearing an apron that proclaims your love of canines? Man, feline. I didn't know you cared so much." Colin scratched his side. "I feel loved, validated, and appreciated right now. I feel seen."

Theo howled, and Horatio, wearing a matching apron,

chittered wildly as the imps managed to hoist the duo a few inches over the steaming sink.

Xandie grabbed two handfuls of her shoulder length hair and tugged, fighting back the scream building inside. Caving, she dropped her hands and fixed heated eyes on her grandmother. "Fix it. Rescue Theo and Horatio, and you're rehired."

Elspeth opened her mouth, but Xandie held a hand up. "There are conditions. You will share the job with our new wedding planner, and you will run everything through me. Understand?"

Elspeth cleared her throat and blinked her own matching amber eyes at Xandie. "Of course, dearest. Favorite granddaughter. Whatever you wish. It *is* your wedding day after all."

"And lo, there was peace among the Harrow clan again for five minutes," Lila intoned before breaking the somber moment with a giggle. "Can you clear the infestation of devilish imps away? Right now? I have a bakery full of customers to bake for."

"With pleasure." Elspeth cracked her knuckles, reached into her green jogging pants pocket, and withdrew a small purple drawstring bag. "I always carry blessed chalk dust, just in case."

"In case of what?" Holly shuffled over until she peeked out from behind Lila.

"In case she can carry out quick raids of mayhem and carnage, of course." Lila snorted.

"I don't care what you're doing. I don't want boiled feline. Hurry up." Xandie stomped her foot.

Opening the bag, Elspeth drew out a handful of the dust and threw it at the imps. Lunging forward in a move that belied the advanced age she always lied about, Elspeth grabbed the rope as the imps holding it froze. "See? No harm done."

"How can you say that? Have you seen me, Librarian?" Theo wailed as Elspeth swung the prisoners back onto the bench.

"At least you aren't furry soup." Xandie unwrapped the rope and tugged off the apron as Elspeth victory twerked around the island counter.

"Your wedding will be amazing. Stupendous. Other witches will be green with jealousy that the Harrow clan has such a magnificent planner as myself," Elspeth crowed.

"I'll regret this for the rest of my life, won't I?"

Holly nodded. "However long that will be, after you end up murdering Elspeth for wedding-related atrocities."

Xandie had an awful feeling her cousin wasn't wrong. Chaos and mayhem equaled Elspeth Harrow. She just needed to get through the next few days. One step at a time, without killing anyone... Easier said than done in Point Muse. The murder capital of the supernatural world.

TWO

"Really? A bible?" Elspeth sneered, top lip curled above her dentures. "I for one would never presume to name anything nonreligious a bible. That's my compassionate, empathetic side." The elderly witch blew lavender bangs out of the way.

"Wedding bible. Wedding. Not *the* bible." A woman dressed in a no-nonsense baby pink suit with boxy shoulders and scraped back greyish-blonde hair glared at Elspeth with watery, pale blue eyes. She hoisted a thick metal-bound book in the air and pumped it up and down a few times like a gym fanatic. "This has everything we will ever need to plan Ms. Meyers' wedding."

Rolling her eyes, Elspeth picked at an orange-painted nail. "What evs. I've got it all handled. I told you. You just need to sit and look competent, while I handle the heavy lifting."

"Look competent?" the woman hissed, crowding close to Elspeth, her wedding book clasped tight to her chest. "I am Noelle Amore. The pre-eminent expert in supernatural wedding planning. I am *the* Point Muse go-to for weddings.

Not the wicked witch, who's spent more time destroying than planning social events."

Elspeth wiped her face. "Say it, don't spray it."

"Argh," the planner screeched and lifted her book overhead, looking all the while like she wanted to smite Elspeth.

"Why don't we all calm down. I'm sure Ms. Harrow has some amazing ideas—*not including vampire elephants*—that we could work into our plans." A tiny, plump woman, with coarse brown hair that billowed out from her head like she'd stuck a finger in an electricity socket, stepped between the warring women. She carefully pried the planner's grasp from the book and cradled it. "Why don't I keep an eye on this while we calm down and have some delicious food our bridesmaid baker has prepared." The little woman returned to her chair and carefully placed the book in front of her as she sat.

"Thanks, Felicity," Xandie whispered from across the table. "I thought Noelle would take Elspeth down with that tome."

Felicity smiled weakly. "Ms. Amore can be a little dramatic. But she gets the job done."

"She's always been that way, even at school. Used to call her tornado Amore." Winifred, Xandie's aunt and Holly's mother, placed a hot chocolate in front of Xandie and patted her niece's back. "I thought you might need this." Winifred tugged off the apron that barely fit around her curvy frame. "Lila's finishing up some orders and will be here in a minute. And who knows where that banshee daughter of mine is. But I'm here for moral support." Winifred patted her tight, fire engine red curls back into place and winked.

"Thanks, Aunt Winnie. I'm going to need all the support I can get.

"That's why I'm here, doll face. Me and the big boy here have you covered. No wedding blood will be shared. No sacrifices too great for the Harrow clan." Colin pranced out from underneath the table, followed closely by the large, black hellhound, Nash.

"Cake," Nash growled, tiny little flames springing to life in his dark eyes.

"Ix-nay on the ake-cay." Colin flipped a paw at Nash's nose. He turned back to Xandie. "I absolutely do not enforce his stance of being fed cake. I am here of my own free will to help and have not in any way been bribed or influenced by any other Harrows." He panted at the end of the sentence and sprawled on the floor. "Geez, responsibility's exhausting."

"Very convincing, pug." Lila placed a decadent, *devil-may-care-but-I-don't* brownie in front of Xandie. "Here, eat this. Might help you get through the cake tasting later."

"Oh, you are a goddess of baking." Xandie picked up the brownie and closed her eyes, inhaling the rich chocolate scent.

"No." The wedding planner forgot her bickering with Elspeth and lunged forward, slapping the brownie out of Xandie's hand. The baked delight flew through the air and landed with a splat in front of Colin.

"It's manna from heaven." He opened his mouth wide, about to gobble the entire slice down, until Nash growled from behind him.

"Oh, yeah. Can't forget my wedding buddy." Colin broke the brownie in half and shoved the other portion at the hellhound. "It kills my soul to do that, but anything for you, pal. I call dibs on the next thrown baked good. Odds are high it will happen again soon." He pulled his brownie potion back under the table. "We'll wait and pounce when the food hits the ground."

"How dare you attack my favorite granddaughter, the only one providing me with wedding planning joy?"

Noelle glared around the bakery, causing the watching customers to duck their heads. The irate woman stared back at Elspeth. "She has a cake tasting today. We don't want to pollute her tastebuds. Plus, she has a wedding dress to fit into. No cake until I say." The planner turned and narrowed her gaze on the bride, waiting for a response.

Xandie nodded slowly before she mouthed, *What the?* at her cousin.

"Cake hater." Lila coughed into her hand to cover her words. She turned and waggled her eyebrows. "All the drama brings the customers, at least."

Xandie glanced around. A customer filled every seat in the bakery, people even crowding around the unlit stone hearth that dominated one wall. Two long couches set back from the old-fashioned hearth had customers squeezed in like sardines. Everyone wanted a ringside seat for the drama. Even the young man with the buzz cut had turned up again, except this time he squeezed into a shadowy far corner and had his head down, not paying attention to the drama unfolding. Xandie's mayhem early warning system pinged in her head. With such entertaining shenanigans unfolding, who wouldn't want to watch? Why was buzz cut guy so different?

The bakery door slammed open, framing the well-preserved brassy redhead in her fifties, who posed with a hand on one hip. "How darling is this bakery? Heart's Delight?" The woman clapped her hands and giggled. "I already have my heart's delight with my sweetie. But this is such a cute little concept."

A tall, slim man with blond hair and a designer suit stood behind the woman. "We need to be at the counter to order, Gigi."

"Of course." Gigi trilled a laugh and sauntered into the bakery. Her frothy mint tea-dress swirled around her knees as she took a step in matching heels. "Malcolm, order me a quad venti white mocha Frappuccino. There's a good boy. I need to take in the ambience of this cute little store." Gigi spun around, oohing and aahing.

Sighing, the slim man headed to the counter. "Could I please have a…"

Lila held up her hand. "Sorry to stop you, but I heard the order. Unfortunately, I can only do a mocha Frappuccino."

Malcolm shrugged. "That's what she gets for visiting a small town. I'll get the Frappuccino and a large latte to go." The man turned to watch Gigi as she spun around.

"Your friend seems energetic," Lila commented as she filled the order.

"Not my friend. Employer. Actually, my employer's fiancée. He's outside on the phone. It's quiet out there." He gestured outside the bakery where a man paced, talking excitedly on the phone.

Elspeth glared at the spinning woman and stepped around her. Catching a glimpse of Malcolm's gesture, her eyes followed and widened as she stared at the older man on the phone. The wicked witch's body stiffened for a few moments, like a statue in the midst of a moving tableau.

Xandie shared a confused glance with Lila and her aunt Winifred. For once in her life, Elspeth looked like a stunned rabbit. And the wicked witch of Point Muse had never resembled a prey animal in her life.

Jerking out of her dazed stupor, Elspeth ripped her gaze

away from the man outside and sniffed. "I'm bored. You know what happens when I'm bored. Colin, you're with me." Elspeth snapped her fingers, and the pug waddled out from underneath the table. Pulling herself together, Elspeth took off at a quick pace toward the kitchen and the back-alley exit.

"What about the cake tasting?" Xandie bellowed at her grandmother.

"I'll check my schedule."

"Man, what's up with the Jekyll and Hyde act?" Colin panted as he padded past Xandie. "Wait up, I'm not as fast as I used to be." He crowded in behind Elspeth as they disappeared into the kitchen.

"What's all that about? She's in the middle of a spat with the planner, then looks outside and disappears?" Not normal Elspeth behavior. Her grandmother had never met an argument she couldn't win. Why run off now?

Winifred grimaced at Xandie. "It's Mother. Who knows what goes through her head any given day?"

Lila shook herself and handed Malcolm his order. "There's your order and the drama's for free."

"I've got my own drama queen to corral." He nodded his thanks and spoke softly to the still spinning woman before they headed back outside. People shifted in their seats, unsure about the abrupt end to their entertainment. Xandie spotted buzz cut guy staring straight at Malcolm and Gigi as they left. He noticed Xandie watching and dropped his gaze, shifting back into the shadows. Playing a *don't-see-me* game with the rest of the bakery...? Or maybe just the Harrows. *Curious and curiouser.*

Lila joined her family watching Gigi juggle her drink and dance around the older man, who shooed her away. "Isn't that the guy with amber eyes from the parade?"

The same man from the parade who'd also had an argument on the Library's dock with Elspeth weeks ago. Why was Elspeth so wary of him? And when had she ever been scared off by anyone?

This doesn't bode well for a mayhem free wedding. What kind of threat would make the wicked witch flee...

THREE

"Do you think she'll show?" Xandie nibbled on a nail as she glanced up and down Main Street.

Miranda Harrow, Xandie's mother, pursed her lips and shrugged. "It's on her if she doesn't. Plus, you get quiet time at the cake tasting. I'd call it a win-win situation." She linked arms with Xandie. "And we get quality mother-daughter time as well."

A smile slowly spread across Xandie's face. "You know what? You're right. A stress-free tasting is just what we need. Zach's going to try to make it, but he's snowed under with paperwork. As long as the cake has honey, he doesn't care what flavor it is."

"There you go. No stress." Miranda winked and focused amber eyes on the wedding planner and her assistant, Felicity. Noelle shook her wedding bible at Felicity and paced up and down the cobblestone pavement in front of Sinful Desserts café.

"The planner seems to be strung a tad tight."

Rolling her eyes, Xandie unlinked her arm from her mother's and smoothed her frizzy brown hair off her face.

"She likes a schedule and guards her wedding bible ferociously. Zach thinks she balances out Elspeth's illogical craziness."

Noelle spun and pointed at Xandie. "And where is our groom?"

"He has to work but will try to make the appointment." Miranda raised an eyebrow. "Surely Xandie's opinion has equal sway?"

Go, Mom. Xandie bit back a smirk. Her mother, a fierce warrior in looks and deed, Miranda Harrow, Elspeth's oldest daughter, stood a slim five foot ten inches and every single inch muscled and honed for action. With the same amber eyes and frizzy long brown hair as her daughter, Miranda had disappeared from Xandie's life when she was five. Chased by a supernatural killer, Miranda had thrown herself off a cliff outside of Point Muse to save her daughter. Her mother had survived but had suffered amnesia. Picked up by a shadowy government organization, she'd been forced to work with them as an assassin and black ops agent for years, until her memory started coming back. Now she split her time between Point Muse and the Harrows, and Portland, Maine, where Xandie's father, Nicholas Meyers, lived.

"I find the couple's wedding connections fare better when both sides are equally invested in a joint decision." The planner ground her teeth and used a fist to bang on the dessert shop door. "I said one o'clock exactly. They were closing the shop to everyone but us. Now it's five minutes past one. The delay is unacceptable." Noelle raised a fist again but lowered it quickly when the door opened.

Ruby Devlin poked her head out and grinned at Xandie through thick black bangs. "Ready to sugar up, Meyers?"

Xandie snorted, then grinned. "When do I ever turn

down sugared offerings of goodness? It's all zero calories, right?" Giggling, she crossed into Sinful Dessert's marble domain.

Ruby's twin sister, Lara, stood next to a large table set up with platters of colorful cake slices. Lara clapped her hands. "We at Sinful Desserts are delighted to be providing the Harrow–Braun bridal party with our catering services." Lara beamed and gestured for the party to take a seat.

"Meyers," Xandie mumbled as she dropped into a chair next to her mother, who'd chosen to have a seat against the wall, facing the room.

Ruby waved Xandie's comment away. "Yeah, Meyers. But when you get down to it, you're a Harrow to the bone."

"Plus, Grandmother Delilah says the Harrow genes eat and kill everything else." Lara smirked.

Delilah Devlin and Elspeth had a hate-on-hate relationship and were enemies from way back. A while ago, they'd semi buried the hatchet—*not in each other's backs*—and were coexisting in the same town in guarded neutrality. Which meant they sniped at each other and conducted prank wars that didn't end up devolving into bloody fighting.

Noelle slapped her wedding book on the table and glared at the twins. "We have a schedule. Get this show on the road, Devlins."

Felicity cleared her throat. "She means if we could start the tasting, that would be great."

"We assumed you'd wait for the other members of your tasting party?" Lara raised an eyebrow.

Ruby backed her sister up with an emphatic nod. "Like the wicked witch of Point Muse?"

Baring teeth, Noelle growled. "My schedule waits for no one. And that includes that wedding planner wannabe."

"Wannabe ain't in my dictionary." Elspeth wandered out of the Devlins' kitchen, munching on a slice of cake. "This triple chocolate, honey, raspberry ripple is to die for."

"Yeah, the bear will love the honey. Just don't expect any cake to be left standing." Colin trotted out from behind Elspeth, chocolate cake crumbs smeared over his cream-colored furry muzzle.

Carly, the Devlins' poodle, took a step to the side to avoid Colin smearing her immaculate white fur.

"I see you decided to show up. There's no need. Everything is under my control."

"No surprises there, when the control freak is in charge." Elspeth sauntered up to the planner and tapped the wedding bible.

"Don't. Touch. My. Book." Noelle gritted her teeth and took a step forward.

"Bring it, control freak." Elspeth cackled and clapped her hands. Shadows trickled in from every corner of the dessert shop, writhing on the floor like black snakes. The shadows curled around Elspeth's orange-colored, combat-boot-shod ankles before inching up her legs and coating her like a shadowy hooded cape. Her amber eyes gleamed from the pitch black of the hood. "I'll even give you the first shot. Winner takes the wedding."

"Hey." Xandie sat up and glared at the women. "No wagering on my wedding. I told you. Both of you are planners. No throwdown. It's cake tasting time." Xandie thumped the table for emphasis.

Lifting her chin, Noelle turned away from Elspeth and focused on the table. "You're the client. Carrying out your wishes is my job." She looked up from the table and frowned. "I said six choices. I only count five here. This is unacceptable."

"Gosh. I am so sorry." Ruby exchanged a puzzled glance with her sister, and both rushed into the kitchen.

"She's really a people person, isn't she?" Elspeth snickered and let her shadowy cape dissolve.

"Mother." Miranda's one word carried a wealth of warning.

"You're all-party poopers." Elspeth flounced into a chair on the other side of Xandie and across from the planner's assistant.

Felicity offered a strained smile. "Wedding planning is a high stress job. Tempers can fray."

"Especially when services you ordered aren't supplied properly." Noelle tapped her foot and checked her watch.

Ruby and Lara rushed out with plates in hand. "Sorry. The triple chocolate, honey, raspberry ripple cake wasn't where we thought." Ruby placed a cake down on the table, and Lara followed suit with multiple plates and forks.

Snatching up her book, Noelle uncapped her pen and opened up a page marked cake. "First, there is a straight fruitcake base with chocolate ganache frosting." She nodded at the twins who served a slice of cake to everyone at the table.

Xandie forked up a small mouthful and chewed. It wasn't bad, but it wasn't decadent chocolate enough for her. She laid her fork across the plate and swallowed.

"Be honest, Ms. Meyers. We might actually escape here ahead of schedule if you do." The planner tapped her pen on paper as she waited for the bride's decision.

Honesty and Harrows don't normally mix. Xandie slid a sideways glance at her grandmother. Honest answers were definitely in short supply when it came to Elspeth Harrow. Xandie still couldn't shake the feeling that something bad was coming and Elspeth knew exactly what.

"Ms. Meyers?"

Clearing her throat, Xandie shook her head. "I don't like fruitcake, and there wouldn't be enough honey for my fiancé." When it came to bear shifters, the more honey, the better.

"No more fruit choices." Noelle snapped her fingers at Felicity, who shifted multiple cake plates out of the way. "Two choices left." The planner consulted her list. "Honey, white chocolate, and triple chocolate raspberry honey ripple. Proceed."

Colin bumped against Xandie's chair and whispered loudly, "Oi. Wedding girl. If you're not snacking on those fruitcakes, how about you shift them my way? Waste is bad." Colin fluttered his dark, beady eyes at Xandie.

"Have at it, pug. Don't blame me when you get a headache or blocked up from the fruitcake." Xandie dragged the fruitcake plates back to her side of the table and handed them down to the ravenous pug.

"Thanks, kid. You're a doll, not the bridezilla Elspeth said you were."

"Yeah, yeah." Taking a deep breath, Xandie turned back to the impatient wedding planner.

"Are we finally ready now?" She frowned at Xandie. "I hope you're taking this seriously. Finding the right flavor of wedding cake can make or break a wedding."

Elspeth snorted. "Please. It's a cake. Slap a boatload of chocolate on top and swamp it in honey and the bride and groom will be happy. There's nothing to it."

"It is the cornerstone of the wedding. A pivotal part of the planning. Which you would know if you were a real wedding planner, and you're not. You're a fake." Noelle hissed the last word at Elspeth.

"Fake? You're calling me fake?" Elspeth surged to her

feet, lips peeled back from her dentures. The sound of glass shattering in the kitchen drove Ruby and Lara out of the room.

"Mother. We talked about this." Miranda's no-nonsense voice broke the tension again, and she glared until Elspeth subsided back into her chair.

Xandie took the opportunity to grab a plate and take a bite. "Honey white chocolate." Xandie swallowed and then licked her lips.... "Not bad." She grabbed the last plate and took a large bite. A combination of bitter and sweet exploded on her tongue. Xandie's eyes rolled, and she groaned before taking another, even bigger, bite.

Snickering, Miranda pointed at the cake. "I think that's the winner."

"Triple chocolate, honey, raspberry ripple." Noelle marked it in her book. She nodded at Felicity. "Please serve everyone else at the table as well. It's good to get multiple opinions."

Nodding, Felicity sliced portions of the cake and carefully placed them on plates before handing a serving to each of the others.

Elspeth crossed her arms, bottom lip pouting. "I've tasted this in the kitchen. Although it's good, it's not my first choice, but as everyone's telling me, it isn't my wedding."

Felicity took a large mouthful and hummed as she chewed. "That's yummy. My vote is the triple chocolate as well."

Noelle slapped her wedding bible on the table jind snatched up a plate. "You have an uneducated palette. As the pre-eminent wedding planner in Point Muse, my cake palate is well-defined." She took a tiny slither of a mouthful before quickly going back for a much larger forkful.

Ruby and Lara rushed back out of the kitchen and collected the empty plates.

Xandie held a thumbs up to the twins. "It's triple chocolate, honey, raspberry ripple for the win."

Lara giggled and elbowed her sister. "We figured that might be your choice. We doubled the honey in the recipe for the police chief."

Felicity beamed. "That's a major decision made. Congratulations." The assistant turned and faced the planner, waiting for a comment.

Noelle grunted and rubbed at her blouse-covered arm with one hand. She dumped the plate on the table. "Is it hot in here?" She stood and loosened a button on her shirt as a tide of red inched up her throat. Noelle coughed to clear her throat and wheezed a breath in and out. "Someone. Turn. The. Heating. Down." She wavered on her feet.

"Noelle? Are you okay?" Felicity jumped up and grabbed her boss by the arm, steadying her.

The planner shuddered and scrabbled at her throat, breath hitching as she tried to suck in air. She pointed at her bag, but her arms dropped to her sides as she slumped to the floor, almost dragging her assistant with her.

Squealing, Felicity lost the fight and sprawled flat on the ground next to her boss. "She's allergic to peanuts and has an epinephrine pen in her bag. Quick, grab it."

"There's no peanuts in any of the cakes. We were very careful," Ruby wailed and held her hands to her mouth.

Lara ran for the counter. "I'll call paramedics and healers."

Miranda leapt up and upended the purse, snatching up the EpiPen. "Here."

"I've never used one before. I have no clue how to do it," Felicity squeaked and held up her hand.

"I've got it." Elspeth yanked the pen from the woman and dropped down next to her co-wedding planner. She jabbed the pen tip against Noelle's outer thigh at a right angle and pushed the injector until it clicked. She held it in place for a few seconds before discarding the pen on the ground behind her.

Xandie and Miranda clustered around, waiting for the injection to start working.

"How long before it works? Because she doesn't seem like she's reacting to it at all." Xandie clutched at her mother's arm, holding tight.

"We should have seen a sign of the symptoms easing by now." Elspeth leaned forward and took the planner's pulse.

Noelle clawed at her throat again, scratching Elspeth's hands as she thumped her upper body against the floor before stilling.

Felicity screeched, a high-pitched squeal that hung in the air. "Is she..."

Taking a pulse again, Elspeth nodded somberly. "She is. The EpiPen should have helped her. Maybe the amount of peanut she'd ingested was too large for her pen to cope with?"

"There's no peanuts. I swear it." Ruby grabbed Xandie, tearing her from Miranda's arms. "Please don't let them blame us. The health department will close us down."

Xandie soothed the youngest Devlin twin. "It'll be okay. At least it wasn't murder."

The crime scene tape flapped in the wind. Xandie huddled behind the rest of the Harrows. "Are they sure?"

Miranda nodded as the deputies drew Felicity to the

side of the shop and had a few quiet words with her. "One of the healers is an old school friend. They found peanuts in the cake she ate from, and her EpiPen had been drained. It was empty when Elspeth injected her. Since Noelle had only filled the prescription a few days ago, the police are leaning toward murder."

Xandie and her two cousins, Lila and Holly, turned and stared at their grandmother.

"Hey. Just because I'm wicked doesn't mean I'm a crazed peanut-obsessed killer." Elspeth shrugged and focused on the covered body as it was loaded into the silent, waiting ambulance.

"You're definitely something else." An elderly man with a greyish-brown comb-over, glittering amber eyes, and a well-loved suit stood a few steps away. "Well, Elspeth, aren't you going to welcome your baby brother permanently home?"

"What?" All the Harrows in attendance yelled the word in unison.

"I knew it. Didn't I tell you?" Xandie crowed to her family. "The amber eyes had been a dead giveaway. He's a Harrow. A mythical male Harrow. Elspeth's younger brother. It's good to be the Queen of I Told You So." Xandie sobered abruptly when she remembered what the fae Lady Rose had said about bad times coming and Harrow on Harrow fighting. It hadn't seemed likely back then... *but now?*

"Edgar. It wasn't me keeping you away from Point Muse." Elspeth gritted her teeth and refused to look at her younger brother.

"Not Point Muse. I could care less for this one-horse town. It's Harrow House I was kept from. And Harrow House I've come back for." Elspeth's brother puffed out his skinny chest. "I've come for my inheritance. Harrow House is half mine, and I want what's due to me."

"*Excuse me?*" At his words, Elspeth finally turned to face her brother, her black, wigged pigtails flapping at the speed she turned. "The house is mine. Our parents left it to me. You weren't even around when they died."

"Correction. They left it to both of us. I've finally come to collect my inheritance, and I have the will and the lawyer to prove it." Edgar sniffed and adjusted the cuffs on his suit jacket. "Basically, pay me my share or I'm moving in. Those are the only choices you have." He gathered the brassy redhead, who'd been busy staring at the crime scene tape, and strolled along Main Street without a care in the world.

"You'll never get Harrow House, Edgar. Do you hear me? Not over my dead body or in this case, *yours,*" Elspeth bellowed before storming in the opposite direction without a word to her family.

Holly's head ping-ponged between the two warring Harrows. "Elspeth has a brother, and he's kicking us out of the house?"

"I'd like to see him try. I bet on Elspeth for the win. And technically he owns only half." Lila scratched the back of her head. "Just in case, you might want to take possession of my foldout couch before your mum or Elspeth does."

"We'll work it out. For now, it might be a good idea to shelve this Harrow drama and focus on the dead wedding planner. "

"Losing Harrow House is important," Holly argued with Xandie.

"What's important is that Xandie's fiancé is taking Elspeth in for questioning." Miranda pointed to the police chief as he intercepted a fuming Elspeth and directed her into the back of a police cruiser.

"There goes world peace as we know it." Xandie sighed and rubbed her forehead. A flicker of movement out of the corner of her eye caught her attention. Across the road, near Lila's bakery, the young man with the buzz cut leaned against the wall and stared fixedly at Edgar Harrow's retreating back. Not at the crime scene or the body being loaded into the ambulance. At Edgar Harrow.

It looks like Elspeth's brother isn't the only one in town with an ulterior motive...

FOUR

Xandie nibbled on her bottom lip and stared at her grandmother through the mirrored glass in the observation room situated beside the interview area. Agatha Braun, police dispatcher and Xandie's future mother-in-law, stood beside her, gaze fixed on her son and Xandie's grandmother.

Aggie shook her head, a worried look on her face. "There's something not right with this. Elspeth—"

"Shhh," Xandie cut her off. "Let's hear what they have to say." Shutting everything else out, she concentrated on the conservation.

"Let me get this right." Zach Braun, police chief, bear shifter, and Xandie's fiancé, blew out a deep, gusty breath. "Noelle Amore was a mean wedding planner, and the wedding planner gods smote her." He read directly from a small notebook.

Elspeth nodded. "Or smited. I'm not the grammar police."

"How about we ignore the fact there are no wedding planning gods and you tell me exactly what happened?"

"You can't handle the truth," Elspeth bellowed and

clambered to her feet with a cackle. "I'll never get bored of saying that."

"I'll definitely get bored of hearing it," Zach muttered under his breath.

"I'm not deaf, bear. Don't you sass me." Elspeth pointed a finger at the police chief. Pink electricity flickered over the tip of a small silver cap fitted to the tip of her finger. "My own version of wearable tasers. I've even got a buyer set up. Want to be my first victim...I mean test subject?" The wicked witch beamed, dentures gleaming.

"Stop trying to change the subject and distract me. This is a murder. A murder connected to your granddaughter's wedding. This. Is. important. Talk, Elspeth." Zach thumped the tabletop for emphasis.

"That's the point. *Harrow wedding.* This is an attack on the whole entire Harrow family. *Me.*" Elspeth slapped her bony chest and paced up and down the length of the interview room. Combat boots smacked at the linoleum floor. Black pigtails swung. Shadows congealed in all four corners of the room, surging in time to her outbursts.

"So, you're saying you are supposed to be the target, not Noelle Amore?"

Elspeth rolled her eyes. "Try following along, shifter. Amore was a nasty wedding planner with a capital N. A mean girl at school to my Winifred and a mean wedding planner. Anyone could have offed her. This is about derailing a Harrow wedding."

"Meyers and Braun actually," Zach corrected.

"Meyers. Harrow. Same thing." Elspeth waved a hand airily.

"Not to those getting married." The police chief cleared his throat. "Did you have a grudge against the wedding planner?"

"Please. I would have driven that no talent hack to quit in the next twenty-four hours. She was a nonstarter. I told you this is a ploy to stall the wedding and get at me. Moi." Elspeth paused her pacing. "This is an attack on the Harrow clan. Where do your loyalties lie?"

Sighing, the chief stood and gathered his paperwork. "Fine, I'll play your game. Who is spearheading this murderous affront against you?"

"Not me. All Harrows." Elspeth paused dramatically, as shadows raced from every corner and coalesced around her like a dark cloud of doom. "Edgar Harrow. My younger brother. He's in town to steal Harrow House and take all the other Harrows down. It's a hate crime."

"A hate crime against Harrows caused by a Harrow?"

"Exactly." Elspeth nodded. All emotion leached from her face and voice. "He wants what he willingly threw away, and he won't get it. Not if I have anything to say about it."

Aggie suddenly nudged Xandie in the side, breaking her concentration. "See what I mean?" She nodded at Elspeth. "She's discombobulated, and that's not like her. She's normally the one unsettling others."

Hmm, Aggie might be right. Elspeth loved dramatics, but if Xandie looked closer, the shaking hands, pale skin, and flat, emotionless eyes screamed out worried. "That old man is really a Harrow, isn't he?"

Aggie sighed and faced Xandie. "Elspeth has a past. When she talks of enemies and nemesis, she isn't exaggerating. Our wicked witch has a talent for rubbing people the wrong way."

"But you don't think it's a past enemy of Elspeth's."

"No. I don't know if Edgar is capable of murder, but

Elspeth's right. The murder is personal and connected to the Harrows or she wouldn't be so off kilter."

"Have you met Edgar before?" The idea of an estranged brother coming to town after decades of silence, wanting to take your home, would be enough to put anyone off their game, including Elspeth.

"Once. Shortly after his wife died. He had a little baby, and Elspeth's parents refused to see him. They left soon after that. All I know is that the police in Point Muse at that stage were still looking for him. I don't think she even knew he had come back."

"And?" Xandie knew there was something else coming.

"He swore he'd get even with his family." Aggie shrugged and met Xandie's gaze with a worried one. "What if he's decided it's time?"

Xandie patted her soon-to-be mother-in-law on the muscular, bear shifter shoulder. "Then we stop him. It's that simple."

"I hope so."

The scrape of a chair against the floor dragged their attention back to the interrogation room. Zach moved across the room to wrench open the door. Xandie and Aggie quickly exited the observation room.

"You won't take me alive, copper," Elspeth yelled and jogged past Zach into a wide-open area with desks currently occupied by Zach's younger twin brothers, Caleb and Riley, and his younger sister, Melody, along with the Devlin twins, Miranda, and Felicity, the wedding planner's assistant.

"You weren't under arrest, Elspeth. It was an interview, over the death of Noelle Amore," Zach snapped as he followed her.

"I can't believe she's dead." Sobs suddenly racked Felicity's square shoulders.

"Yes." Elspeth ground to a halt next to the assistant and rearranged her face from gleeful to sympathetic. "It's very sad, a wedding planner murdered like that." She patted Felicity awkwardly on top of the head.

"Murder?" Felicity jolted her head back and dislodged Elspeth's hand, the assistant's now dry eyes wide open.

"What?" Lara Devlin gasped.

"I swear we didn't poison your cake," Ruby Devlin wailed and hid her head in her twin sister's dark hair.

"Settle down. We have no proof, yet this is an official murder. We're waiting for tests to come back from our healers and crime scene team. Until then, go home." The police chief fixed the occupants of the room with a steely blue gaze. "No one leaves town." He turned on the spot and stomped into his office, slamming the door shut.

Her poor honey-loving, furry boy was not a happy camper. Xandie made a mental note to stop by Lila's bakery for some honey buns.

"What makes you think it's murder, Mother?" Miranda Harrow's calm, cool tones cut through the babble in the police station.

Elspeth smiled at her eldest daughter, like she was a prized student. "The only one at the table with a peanut allergy was Amore. The killer could have slipped peanut oil into all of the cake tasting plates. It didn't matter which one as long as the planner tasted some. Everyone else wouldn't have reacted to the oil."

Felicity gulped. "Noelle hated cake. She only ever tasted the one the bride and groom picked." She looked stunned for a moment. "I wasn't the only one who knew that. Noelle's been in the business for years. Plenty of people knew her procedures."

"Of course, dear. No one suspects you." Elspeth rubbed

Felicity's head again. "It would be easy enough to grab Amore's purse and exchange her EpiPen for an empty one. The woman dumped her bag everywhere. She only cared about that wedding bible."

Elspeth stared at the late wedding planner's prized possession, currently on the table in front of Felicity. Dragging the thick tome closer to her, the assistant covered it with her hand. "It's my job now to protect it. It's her legacy to Point Muse weddings." Her face crumpled again as she sobbed, her cries growing in volume. "What am I going to do now? Noelle was supposed to train me. I'm her protégé, and now I haven't even got a job."

"Priorities," Xandie muttered.

"It's the younger generation. They're whacked."

"Is that a professional term, Deputy Melody?" Xandie teased Zach's younger sister.

"An observation. Felicity is only in her early twenties. She's got a few years yet until she hits our jaded ages."

"We're in our mid-twenties. Okay, maybe late twenties. We aren't much older than her," Xandie protested.

"Experience with Elspeth counts like dog years. Plus, with Point Muse being the murder center of the supernatural world, we're as old as the hills." Melody nodded sagely.

"If the peanut gallery will pipe down, I have an important announcement to make." Elspeth drew herself up. "My heart has been moved by this poor little lamb's plight. Therefore, I am taking over the Harrow-Braun wedding as sole planner. I'm rehiring Felicity. The wedding and Felicity's job will go on." Elspeth reached over her new assistant and yanked the bible out from under her hands. "As such, the bible now belongs with me. I am declaring an all-hands-on-deck wedding meeting at Harrow House tonight. Be there or be a toad. So say I." Elspeth grabbed Felicity under the arm and tried to heave her upright. Giving up, she grunted at the assistant. "Shake a leg, girl. We've got a Harrow wedding the plan."

"Is there any point reminding you it's a Meyers-Braun wedding?"

"Nope. Tootles, losers." Elspeth propelled Felicity out of the room.

The tension lessened and Aggie sniffed. "Well, then. Meeting at the house tonight. I'll bring honey cakes. We'll need the sugar to get through. Now, everyone out. I've got work to do."

Aggie speared a glance at Xandie. "Keep an eye on her and Edgar. We don't need Harrows in the morgue or a jail cell anytime soon."

"Need a ride back to the Library, sweetie?" Miranda smiled down at her daughter.

Kind of nice having her mom around again, even if she split her time between Andrews with Xandie's father and Point Muse. Returning her smile, Xandie shook her head. "I want to speak with Zach, and then I'll walk back to the bakery. Lila will give me a lift home."

Nodding, Miranda waved goodbye and headed out.

Pausing in front of Zach's office door, she eased it open and leaned against the doorjamb, inspecting her belea-guered fiancé. Normally his sandy-colored hair tended toward the shaggy side. But his mother or Elspeth had nagged the bear into getting a haircut. It still needed more trimming but was much better than normal. His uniform sported creases like he'd slept in it, and his light blue eyes were slightly bloodshot. "Are you sure you want to marry into the Harrow family?"

"Meyers," Zach snapped out automatically before flashing his fiancée a wry smile. "Sounds quiet out there."

Xandie sauntered toward her fiancé and climbed onto his lap, settling in. "Elspeth has rehired Felicity and taken control of the wedding and the bible. Apparently, there's a crisis meeting at Harrow House tonight."

"Yay for us."

Smothering a giggle into his muscled shoulder, Xandie gripped her bear shifter in a tight squeeze before releasing him. "Your mom's bringing honey cakes, and I might even get some honey buns from Lila's."

"Well, in that case, I'll be there."

Xandie listened to his heartbeat for a few moments. "It *is* murder, isn't it?"

"Looking that way."

"And once again, Elspeth's the prime suspect. I think our wedding's jinxed."

Zach brushed a floating kiss over Xandie's frizzy hair. "Elspeth's always a suspect. We could elope if that's what you want."

He isn't wrong on both counts. But do I want to deal with the fallout if we elope? "We need to solve this before it gets out of hand." Xandie sat up and pressed a kiss to Zach's nose before clambering off. "First step is finding out what Edgar Harrow wants and what he's prepared to do to get it."

"Try not to find any more bodies. You'll get a reputation."

Snorting, Xandie slipped out the door. "I'm part Harrow, remember? Already have a reputation."

"Meyers soon-to-be Braun...*I hope.*"

Xandie left with Zach's words still hanging in the air. She hoped so too... All she needed to do was swing into Sherlock Librarian mode and track the killer down. Be they Harrow or not... *Easier said than done.*

FIVE

"Do we have snacks?" Colin sniffed around the Harrow House sitting room. "Mystery-solving meetings should have snacks. It's like a rule."

Lila used her toe to poke the pug's stomach. "It's a meeting about a wedding. Not a mystery solver anonymous."

"There should still be snacks." Colin dropped at Elspeth's feet with a sigh.

"Don't worry, sweetie. Where there is Winifred, there's snacks." Elspeth cooed over her doggy minion before straightening. "Right. Everyone sound off."

"Are we in the army, now?" Xandie muttered to her cousin, Holly, sprawled next to her on the sofa.

"Depends on who you talk to." Amelia, Lila's mother, checked her watch. "Could we get on with the show? I have a patient on the way."

Lila's mother was an animal empath and the town veterinarian. The middle Harrow sister, Amelia stood tall at five feet ten inches and was as skinny as her daughter, Lila,

39

was curvy. A grayish-brown streaked ponytail swung as she lifted the arm wearing her watch into the air. "Tick tock, people. If you're waiting for the boys, they're in the kitchen with Winifred. I've vote we start without them."

"Dirty, rotten cheaters." Colin scrambled to his feet. "Those snacks are mine." He waddled out.

"Go ahead, Mother. We can fill in Matthew and Zach on what they need to do later," Miranda calmly ordered.

"Fine." Elspeth cleared her throat and dragged Felicity up from the loveseat where she sat. "This is the official appointment of Felicity as my number two." Elspeth frowned as her granddaughters snickered. "What's so funny about number two?"

Lila cleared her throat. "Apologies. A little toilet humor. Please continue."

Glaring, Elspeth pushed Felicity back into the loveseat. "This is serious business afoot. We only have a little while to bring this together. We need laser focus to produce the most magical event of the year." She paused, staring at her daughters and granddaughters. "Got it?" Elspeth barked.

"Yep."

"Yes."

"Loud and clear."

Three granddaughters slapped out an automatic reply, their responses ingrained.

Their mothers smiled at the reaction.

"No nonsense." Elspeth snapped her fingers. Felicity rushed to open the late planner's wedding bible and held it up.

"Job allocations. This is extremely important, and you lay-abouts aren't going to heap all the work on me." Elspeth turned to Felicity but froze as a sharp jolt shook Harrow House.

"Whoa." Xandie grabbed the arm of the sofa as the jolts lasted for a few seconds longer. "What's that?"

Elspeth crossed to a wall and rubbed it gently. "Maybe it's excited about the wedding? Been a while since we've had one."

Zach, with Lila's boyfriend, Matthew, close behind, poked their heads into the sitting room. "Everyone okay?"

Snorting, Elspeth dropped her hand from the wall. "Of course, we're fine. The house probably has indigestion."

"Digestive problems?" Holly frowned and rubbed her chest. "Actually, I might have indigestion too."

"You're a hypochondriac," Elspeth snapped. "The house is fine. The wedding isn't. Now let's—" The words were interrupted by a series of loud bangs. The floor rolled from side to side, and everyone grabbed a stationary object and held on tight. A roaring noise like a jet flying low overhead filled the room.

"It's an earthquake," Holly bellowed and launched herself from the couch, scrambling for a doorway. "Quick, under here."

Elspeth rolled her eyes. "It's not an earthquake."

Zach crowded in behind Holly. "Over here, Xandie. Holly's right. Safer under here."

The house shook wildly for a few seconds more. The tinkling of broken glass along with heavy thumps sounded throughout the house.

Her bear shifter might have a point. Xandie rose from the couch, carefully standing as the house's shaking subsided. "I think it's almost over."

"I keep telling you. It's the house just having a conniption fit. Nothing to stress about." Elspeth flipped her pigtail over her shoulder. The house stilled completely, the silence deafening. "See?" Elspeth raised an eyebrow. "What did I tell you?"

Multiple loud knocks echoed from the front door.

Screeching, Holly jumped behind Xandie's fiancé and placed a hand on her chest. "My heart can't handle the stress."

"It's just the front door," Xandie snickered and slid past fraidy cat Holly to open the door, staring back at her family from over a shoulder. "It's probably just wedding stuff."

"It's really not."

A man's reedy voice shocked Xandie into dragging her gaze back to the front. Edgar Harrow with his well-worn suit and glittering amber eyes stood on the porch. "I told you, Elspeth. I own half the property. Even Harrow House knows it, otherwise you'd never be able to open that door."

Elspeth muscled her way through her quiet family to stand next to Xandie. "And I told *you*. Over my dead body." She glared at her brother. "Or yours. I'm not picky."

"Ahem." A tall man with thick, wavy blond hair and blinding white teeth stepped forward and glanced at a metal bound notebook in his hand before stowing it away out of sight. "My client, Mr. Harrow, has a rightful right to claim half of this house." He looked at Elspeth's brother for reassurance before continuing. "As such, you, Elspeth Lilith Harrow, have an obligation to either provide half of Harrow House for my client's use or produce a fair and equitable amount to be paid out for his half." The man ground to a halt and stared expectantly at Xandie and her grandmother.

"Rightful right?" Xandie grimaced. Better words could have been chosen.

Lila popped up next to Xandie, munching on some popcorn. "Entertainment and a snack. This meeting is turning out great."

Ignoring her granddaughter's antics, Elspeth glared at the now sweating man in front of her. "Who are you, little man?"

The man drew himself up and in a grand tone introduced himself. "I am James Neville, Esquire. I'm a lawyer, representing Mr. Edgar Harrow." Reaching in his pocket, he drew out a business card and handed it to Elspeth, who threw it over her shoulder without reading.

"Doesn't matter who you are, you're not stepping a foot inside Harrow House. Not one of you. If Edgar wanted to be part of the family, he should have come back years ago. His choice." Elspeth shoved Xandie to the side and tried to close the door, but the lawyer slid his foot in the way and used a hand to push it open again.

"I'm afraid my client has a claim, and you are legally obliged to honor it." Keeping one hand on the door, he reached into his suit jacket pocket and drew out a crumpled wad of papers. "This is a copy of the will, left by Agnes and William Harrow. It details their estate, including Harrow House, is to be left equally to their children. Elspeth Lilith Harrow and Edgar William Harrow."

Elspeth yanked the will out of the lawyer's hand and ripped it to shreds. "This is all a fake-out by Edgar. My parents knew Edgar was a grifter and cheat. They would never allow him to inherit. This is one of his cons."

Gasping, Edgar shook his head. "Baseless lies. Our parents threw me out because they couldn't stand my sainted late wife, Sylvie. That's why we left. And *I* am a successful businessman."

"You deal in flimflam. And there was no kicking you out. You ran before the police came knocking."

"Now, now, dearest." A brassy redhead sauntered up to the edge of the Harrow House steps and stopped with one hand on her hip. She patted her red hair. "Such a shock, having you turn up after so long. I'm sure your big sister wants to do what's right."

"What's right?" Shadows leapt from Elspeth pigtails and crawled on the side of Harrow House, covering the lavender-colored, Victorian house in black, thick, shadowy paint. "What's right is I have been here for years, looking after the family and the house while you played with vitamins."

Xandie stepped off to the side of the porch and out of Elspeth's blast zone.

Edgar's amber eyes flashed. "I have a legal right to Harrow House, just like you. Blame our parents for this mess." He stepped closer to the front door. "And look, the house isn't doing anything to stop me. It knows I'm right."

"This is my family, my house. You aren't welcome."

The lawyer wiped his palms on his suit pants. "Now, see here, Ms. Harrow…"

Elspeth shoved her hands forward, and the shadows formed a wide, high partition, forcing the lawyer and Edgar back, step-by-step.

The lawyer slipped off the stairs and grabbed hold of Edgar's suit jacket, yanking him back until they both ended up in a suited pile of limbs on the ground.

"And don't come back." Elspeth slammed the door shut. The shadows dissipated with a pop, leaving the faint glow of the porch to illuminate the men in the evening shadows.

"Wow wee." The redhead blew her breath out with a whoosh. "Some temper."

Edgar stood carefully and brushed himself off. "She was prone to tantrums as a child as well."

Crawling around on all fours, the lawyer scrabbled

through the dirt until he found his notebook. He stowed it away and stood. "I'm not cut out for physical confrontations."

"You deal with whatever I pay you to." Edgar glared.

"Honey?" The redhaired woman jerked her head at the porch and Xandie. "We have an onlooker."

Xandie took a step forward. "If you're her brother, then you knew that little act wouldn't work."

"We wanted to give Elspeth a chance before we invoked the courts. Obviously, that was a mistake."

Boy, was it a mistake. Elspeth did not do forgive and forget. Especially when it involved threats. "Why does she think her parents would never leave you something in their will?" Elspeth seemed so certain. There had to be a reason.

"My parents were set in their ways. And they didn't approve of my relationship with Sylvie. They gave me an ultimatum. I left with her." Edgar stared at Xandie with amber, puppy dog eyes. "For a better life. For my love. You understand, don't you?"

Going for the emotional manipulation. Definitely a Harrow trait. Xandie arched an eyebrow. "And if my fiancé, the police chief, ran a check on you?"

Twitching his nose, Edgar dropped Xandie's gaze. "Yes. Well. Youth can interfere with logic. I made some mistakes. But the will is real. Elspeth needs to check her own copy."

"I'm pretty sure she had no clue about you inheriting."

"I'm not surprised. She likes to bury her head in the sand. You can check the study yourself." Edgar sniffed and turned, offering his arm to his girlfriend.

Xandie had to move quickly if she wanted to head off the Elspeth tornado she saw forming in the future. "I can meet you at Mayweather Inn at the bar, tomorrow just before lunch. I won't promise Elspeth will be there, but I will listen to you."

Nodding, he gathered his lawyer and girlfriend and clambered into a black sedan.

Xandie watched as the lawyer gunned the engine, spinning the car's wheels wildly, and left in a hurry. Staring at the car as it disappeared out of view, something caught Xandie's attention. Hard to make out but something...or someone...shifted back into the shadowy forest that bordered Harrow land. Someone watched them. Watched the whole fight unfold on the porch. Normally Xandie's mayhem meter would ping if someone fiendish spied nearby. Why not this time?

"We have an issue." Lila stood framed in the front doorway.

Discarding her suspicions, Xandie faced her cousin. "We always have an issue. Other than a long-lost brother turning up wanting to take Harrow House from Elspeth, what else do we have?"

"Yeah. Elspeth's gone mental. She's finally had the mental break we've all been waiting for. Now we can get rid of her to Eternal Springs Retirement home." Lila held the door open.

"Ever into the breach," Xandie muttered and slipped inside to deal with the issue. Chaos met her gaze. Matthew and Zach were covered in pink goo and stuck to the wall. Winifred stood in front of the men splashing a white liquid on the pink bubblegum material.

"What happened?"

"Elspeth. Mother stormed in and let loose. Harrow House isn't reacting. It's like it shut down. Your Aunt Amelia tried to calm Elspeth and was hit with a sleepy time hex. She's snoring on the floor of the sitting room. The boys went to help, and she gooped them." Winifred splashed a larger amount of the white liquid and waited while the pink goo melted. "This is corn flour and water. It'll deal with the goo. You need to find your mother and Holly. They followed Elspeth."

"This way." Lila led Xandie to the back of the house. "Elspeth screeched something about the study."

"We don't have a study."

"Elspeth's parents did. It's still here, but the house hid it away after they died."

A dull thud sounded, and Xandie veered off to follow the noise. Turning a corner, she found her cousin and mother banging on an old ornate wooden door.

"She locked herself in with magic. And the house won't respond." Holly bit her lip. "Maybe it has a virus?"

"It's in shock. Two heirs on opposing sides, each with a valid claim, will confuse it." Miranda grimaced. "And judging by the way Elspeth flew into a rage, her brother might very well be correct about the will. Obviously, Elspeth had no idea. I think that's why she headed straight for her parents' study. To check."

Xandie pressed her lips together. "Right. We need to deal with this."

"How?" Holly wailed. "She magically locked the door."

"That's why you have me. Remember? The Library makes me immune to most magic." She placed a hand on the doorknob, which turned easily. "Brace yourselves. I'm going in." She flung the door open and stepped into the room.

Leather chairs sat in front of a dark-stained, heavy wooden desk. Bookshelves filled with dusty tomes covered every available wall. And Elspeth stood in the center surrounded by a cloud of white papers that floated around her.

"You okay, Elspeth?" Xandie spoke quietly, not willing to spook the emotional wicked witch.

Elspeth snapped her fingers, and the paper drifted to the ground. She slammed the wooden box on the desk closed and spun to face Xandie. "I don't care what my parents wanted. That man is not stepping a foot in my house." She stamped. "Do you hear me?" She glared around the room before shoving past Xandie on the way out.

"She's gone from denial to anger. She's moving through the stages of grief quickly." Holly, followed by Xandie's mother, stepped into the study. "This place is old school. Definitely not Elspeth's style."

Xandie opened the lid of the brown box Elspeth had abandoned. A crumpled ball of cream paper sat on top of a pile of old faded photos. Drawing out the crumpled paper, Xandie flattened it on the desk. "Last will and testament of Agnes and William Harrow." Xandie scanned the single sheet. "They did leave half the house to him; they also say that he must show an upright character to receive his share of the estate." Xandie looked at her mother. "What does that mean?"

"Whatever behavior got him kicked out of the house, they wanted him to stop it. One of my contacts can look into his history."

"Someone was in the forest as well, watching Elspeth and Edgar fight. At least, I think there was," Xandie amended. "It's getting darker out there, making it harder to see. But shadows don't move unless you're Elspeth."

"I'll have a look. Upgrade our security as well." Miranda frowned. "Who would be interested in a family inheritance argument?"

Xandie picked up a photo of a much younger Elspeth in an old-fashioned dress standing with her arm around a younger boy in a formal suit. The boy, unmistakably, was Edgar Harrow. "That's the question. What else is going on here?" *And who resorted to murder and why...*

SIX

"Are you sure you want to do this by yourself?"

"I'm not by myself. Mom's lurking in the bar some-where, and you're waiting with the van in case we need a quick getaway."

Lila patted her neon-painted bakery van. "The old girl does move quickly when we need her to."

"Okay. You can stop gushing over your bakery death-trap. It's making me feel uncomfortable," Xandie quipped, but her mind was on her upcoming meeting and how much Elspeth would make her pay for it.

"It'll be fine. She'll forgive you...eventually. So, get in there and douse the flames of Armageddon now before we have an extinction level event."

"Always a drama llama." Winking, Xandie took her cousin's advice and headed into Mayweather Inn and her meeting with Edgar Harrow.

"Good morning and welcome to..." Rose Mayweather, descendant of Aphrodite, inn owner and hater of all things Harrow, ground to a halt when she spotted Xandie standing in the foyer. "Oh. It's you." She curled her lip and eyed Xandie's holey jeans.

Sauntering in, her Harrow annoying-others genes spiking, Xandie leaned against the reception desk. "How's it going, Rose?"

"It depends on what chaos you bring." She glared at Xandie. "Your planner has yet to confirm whether you want to book the dining room for your reception. Obviously, Mayweather Inn won't be catering, other than limited hors d'oeuvres."

"Unfortunately, she died. Elspeth's taken over."

Rose recoiled, a horrified expression crossing her face. "No live or dead animals. It's in our contract."

Point Muse residents knew Elspeth far too well. "On that point, we agreed. I'll get Elspeth to contact you. I'm here for a meeting."

"Ah." Rose nodded. "Mr. Harrow. So different from Elspeth. Charming as well." Her hand fluttered over her bra-enhanced chest.

"Okay. Thanks for that information. Can you point me to the Harrow dreamboat before Elspeth hunts us all down?"

"In the bar, first booth on the left." Rose narrowed a glance at Xandie. "Make sure you lock in your reception. Mayweather Inn is an in demand social event provider." She sniffed, dismissing Xandie.

"I'll get right on it. Right after I deal with an explosive situation that has the potential to take out the whole of Point Muse," she muttered under her breath as she pushed the heavy bar door open. Considering it was just before lunch, a surprising number of Point Muse residents were hanging around the bar. Including the sharp-eyed, buzz cut man from

Lila's bakery. The guy got around. Xandie let her eyes drift to the corner of the room where her mother leaned against the bar in shadow. She subtly indicated the guy. Miranda dropped her head a minuscule amount, acknowledging her daughter. Handy sometimes, having a black-ops-experienced mother. Xandie pasted a polite smile on her face and strode up to the booth her great uncle and his lawyer sat in.

"Thanks for meeting me. I'd like to get this sorted out before my wedding and before Elspeth finds out." Xandie slid into the other side of booth.

James Neville, the lawyer, quickly closed his notebook. "I'm sure we all want a satisfying conclusion to this issue. The facts are my client, Mr. Harrow, has a legal right to half of Harrow House or a financial compensation equal to the value of his inheritance." After reciting the words like a learned speech, he folded his hands and stared expectantly at Xandie.

"We had no clue about Elspeth having a brother, let alone him inheriting half of Harrow House."

Edgar tapped the table with buffed nails. "I'm not surprised. My sister has never been one to share her secrets. She gets that from our parents. They were close-mouthed too. That's the reason I left."

"I got the impression you left before the police could arrest you?" That was definitely an Elspeth trait.

"Ha." Edgar slapped the table. "That's what my parents told my deluded older sister. This was all about control of my choice of life partner." He dropped his gaze and traced a worn pattern marked on the weathered tabletop. "Sylvie, my late wife, was a Charis. Her family and the Harrows had feuded for generations. They were low level charisma talents, and my parents looked down on them. Called them grifters."

"Were they?"

"While they had plenty of get rich schemes that never eventuated, they weren't grifters." Edgar's eyes glittered as he lifted his head and focused on Xandie. "My parents forbade me to see Sylvie. I refused, and they kicked me out. So, we left. Left our families and left the town. We found out we were pregnant and planned to come back, but Sylvie, unfortunately, didn't survive the birth. I tried coming back afterward with my son, but my parents weren't interested." He settled back in his seat. "After that, I was too busy providing for my family. Making my mark on the world."

"And you're back now. Why?" Why just before her Elspeth-managed wedding? If he wanted to find time to create maximum mayhem, right before a wedding was the time to do it. And taking out her wedding planner and framing Elspeth? Good way to ruin and disrupt the Harrow clan permanently.

"That's my fault, sugar." The middle-aged brassy redhead tottered toward Xandie on sky high, emerald-green stilettos that matched her tight, green, knee-length dress. "My sweetie and I got engaged not long ago, and I had to see where he's from. He decided to slay two birds with one stone...so to speak." The woman snapped her fingers at the slim man from the bakery, who shoved a chair behind her. The woman settled in with a sensuous wiggle, and Edgar's eyes glazed over.

Xandie fought the juvenile urge to poke her tongue out at the woman's over-the-top sex appeal.

"My, my." The woman giggled. "I do forget myself. I'm Gigi Charming." She leaned forward and held out a pale hand tipped with red-painted nails.

Taking the woman's hand, Xandie gave it a perfunctory

shake before trying to let go. Gigi tightened her grip for a moment, then dropped Xandie's hand.

Gigi frowned, searching Xandie's face for something before smiling sweetly. She waved a hand over her shoulder. "That's my sweetie's assistant, Malcolm. Although he mainly fetches and carries for me. Such a lovely boy."

"My degree in business management put to good use," Malcolm muttered as he placed a dripping glass of water in front of the woman.

Xandie flashed a sympathetic smile at the morose assistant.

"We all know how qualified you are, boy. But the focus is my claim to Harrow House."

"That's the problem. It's not like we can sell the house to pay you off. It's sentient. It has feelings."

"It doesn't have feelings. It's just a house with attitude. If you don't have the guts to get rid of it, just pay me what I want. You're the Librarian. You're probably rolling in cash."

Xandie snorted. She received a stipend into a bank account, monthly, for her expenses but that was it. "Money isn't a Library thing. Surely, we can work something else out. An outcome that works for both sides of the family."

"The only outcome I'll consider is half of Harrow House or the cash equivalent."

"Honey bear. Do you mean we could live in this charming little town?" Gigi clapped her hands and jiggled up and down, nearly taking herself out with her own bouncing body parts. Instead, she knocked over a glass of water, soaking the table, the lawyer, and Xandie.

"Not my notebook!" the lawyer wailed and shot out of the booth, a small damp notebook in hand. "I can't work in these conditions. I'm an artiste. This is intolerable."

Gigi shifted her chair back, accidentally placing it smack in the center of the lawyer's foot.

Howling, he grabbed at the chair and shoved it, and Gigi, forward, until she pressed against the table, her abundant gifts almost overflowing.

The lawyer ignored everyone and hobbled out of the bar.

"I'm so sorry. I'm a clumsy clod."

"You said it." Malcolm dropped a bar towel he'd grabbed over Gigi's over-exposed curves.

Gritting her teeth, Xandie fought not to wiggle in her squidgy, wet jeans. "Accidents happen."

"Not in Point Muse." Edgar slapped the wet table, and water sprayed Xandie's top.

He pointed a finger at his great niece. "This is the type of behavior I'd expect from my sister, not the precious Librarian of the Great Library of Alexandria." Edgar slid out of the booth and yanked Gigi to her feet. "No negotiation. I want my inheritance." He glared at Xandie, then dragged his fiancée from the room, a bored-looking Malcolm trailing behind.

"Hey. I didn't do this," Xandie bellowed. "I'm not Elspeth." But Edgar had already disappeared. Sighing, she stood and slid out of the booth, wincing at the chafing of the wet denim. Her great uncle had a carbon copy of Elspeth's erratic temper. The Point Muse residents around the bar concentrated on their drinks now that the show had finished. All except for the man with the buzz cut. He pushed his untouched drink away and headed for the door.

Making a snap decision, Xandie darted forward and interrupted the man's path. Pretending to trip, she grabbed the man's arm. "Wow. Sorry. Guess I'm clumsy too." Strong arm muscles clenched under her hand.

"No worries. It happens."

The man's deep voice echoed around Xandie, but he kept his head down, not meeting her gaze. There was something about him. "Especially when one gets soaked in water. Even my poor boots were hit. I guess you saw that." Xandie pretended to right herself and dropped her hand away.

"I'm sorry?" The man's head jerked up as he focused over Xandie's shoulder.

"When you were watching us in the booth." Xandie smiled sweetly. "Who wouldn't watch, right?" Xandie took a page out of Gigi's book and trilled a laugh, playing a vapid Librarian with no social skills. "I noticed you because I saw you in the bakery earlier. It almost feels like you're following me, but that's silly talk, isn't it?"

Freezing for a few seconds, the man grunted out a rusty laugh. "It's a small town. There are only a few places to eat and drink. I'll try and keep out of your way if it makes you feel uncomfortable."

His face rippled under his jaw a tiny bit as she watched. She smiled sweetly. "As you said. It's a small town."

Nodding, he left the bar at a fast clip.

What was up with his face? He definitely wore a hex or some kind of glamour. Something that covered or disguised his face. Why would someone need to do that?

"Watch that one." Miranda slid to a stop next to her daughter.

"Why? Is he dangerous?"

"Probably. He has that look."

"You mean, an Elspeth-I'm-about-to-snap kinda look?"

"More like a thousand-yard stare. Someone who's seen action and is ready to act himself, whatever gets thrown his way."

"You think he's military or ex-military?"

"I think he's had training and is here for a reason. Be careful." Miranda winked and blended back into the throng of residents near the bar.

"Great. Now we have military types stalking my wedding." Maybe she should elope, ignore the family squabbles, and go on an early honeymoon. Pushing the door open, Xandie stepped out into the reception area to find Gigi and Rose facing off.

"I'm sure it was just an oversight. Making a bed is quite a basic skill to learn. But hospital corners are always the best choice. If you could send your housekeeping crew up to remake my bed, that would be amazing." Beaming at the inn's owner, Gigi linked her arm through Edgar's and led him out to the front porch.

"That woman is a menace." Rose glared at the front door. "I thought Elspeth was bad, but that woman is worse."

"All that sexy sweetness makes my teeth ache," Xandie admitted.

"It's the fake behavior. Say what you will about Elspeth, she's never sweet or fake." Rose sniffed. "Plus, I'm sure she's only with that poor man for his money. With all the labels she's wearing, I'm surprised he has any cash left."

Maybe there was another reason Edgar needed his inheritance. Xandie made a noncommittal noise.

"And I've heard her whispering on the phone," Rose continued. "She always hangs up when anyone gets too close. I think she's up to something." Rose nodded. "There's a mystery for you to solve that doesn't involve bodies...yet."

"Thanks for the information, Rose. I'll get right on it." Along with solving a murder, planning her wedding, and keeping Elspeth and Edgar from tearing each other apart.

Plenty of time...

SEVEN

"I'm sorry I've been neglecting you, sweetie. It's just this wedding is sucking out all my energy like a parasitic entity living off my wedding planning anxiety. I promise I'll do better." Xandie leaned against a wall in her Library and patted the wood gently.

The chandelier lights overhead flared, then settled into a warm, comforting glow.

"Sounds like you're describing Elspeth, except she's a soul sucking entity in her own right even without a wedding." Lila flapped a hand at her cousin. "But if you supply the chaos, she'll suck it down like a witch dying of thirst."

"She's not that bad." Holly ground to a halt. "Okay, Elspeth is that bad. For some reason, she's obsessed with the wedding."

"Not *the* wedding. My wedding." Xandie thumped her chest. "Mine. Mine. Mine."

"Calm down, bridezilla. Your horns are showing." Elspeth sauntered in, her pink wig of spiral curls slipping down her back. Her matching pink combat boots hit the wooden floor, echoing through the Library. The wicked witch of Point Muse and her bubblegum-pink velour jogging suit glared at her granddaughter. "And it's *our* wedding. O. U. R. S."

"I don't see you marrying my fiancé."

"Ha. The bear shifter should be so lucky." Elspeth slid her hands to her hips and scowled around the room. "I sent out a meeting text this morning. I explicitly stated it was mandatory attendance. Why do I only have the laze-abouts?"

"Three laze-abouts and one fantastic feline."

Theo, Xandie's talking black cat and feline guardian to the Supernatural Great Library of Alexandria, strutted past Elspeth, his tail whipping at her legs. "And I've been promised karaoke. Remember? Karaoke. Put that in your wedding bible."

"I'm here. I'm here." Felicity rushed in, plump cheeks reddened by her hasty progress. "Did someone say karaoke? I have that down as a must-have for the reception. With emphasis on romantic ballads." Felicity flicked through the pages of the thick book until she found what she needed. She tapped the page and nodded. "Yep. First priority is karaoke."

"Oh well. As long as my wedding has karaoke, all is well in the world." Xandie grabbed a bound scroll and shelved it with a pile of others before turning to glare at her cat. "Since when is this wedding about you or Elspeth?"

"Since you turned into a bridezilla." Theo hawked up a furball and dropped it at Xandie's feet. "By the way, I have a parcel coming."

"You have a parcel?" Xandie stared nonplussed at her cat. "You have paws. How do you buy anything?"

"Ever heard of dictation? I ordered matching wedding

outfits for me and Horatio. We will outshine the bridal party. All will see my feline magnificence."

Xandie shuddered. Considering once upon a time Theo had been a hip-flask-guzzling ancient Greek scroll-porn-reading teenager, she didn't hold out much sartorial hope.

Elspeth slapped a hand on Xandie's heavy wooden desk. "Focus, Harrows. We still need to assign jobs if we want this wedding running smoothly."

"When did our grandmother swap bodies with a pod person? Since when does she want things to run smoothly and chaos free?"

"Stuff it, banshee. This is our Harrow reputation on the line."

"And what about your long-lost brother turning up and the wedding planner's death? Doesn't that affect our Harrow reputation?" Lila settled back against the couch as she interrogated her grandmother. "How about for once you tell us what's going on?"

"Nothing is going on, baker girl. Edgar just wants some money." Elspeth curled her lip. "I'll sell something. Easy peasy."

Considering Elspeth had a habit of designing weapons of mass chaos and mayhem, that worried Xandie more than Theo's future karaoke performance. "And the wedding planner?"

"Nothing to do with me." Elspeth shrugged. "Murder happens when you upset people. It's a problem I've never had."

Felicity squeaked. "She wasn't that bad. Noelle was just a little abrasive. Really." She shuffled the book in her arms. "I have a list of jobs that still need doing. Do we assign duties now?"

"Sorry we're late. Murders unfortunately trump wedding planning."

"Not if you listen to your mother." Aggie Braun, matriarch of the Braun clan, shoved past her son and high-fived Elspeth. "Way to remove the competition, Harrow."

"Mom." Zach glared. "Don't egg her on. Murder isn't something to encourage."

Aggie shrugged her muscular shoulders and winked the same colored blue eyes as her son. "I see nothing wrong in removing the competition as long as you don't get caught." Aggie beamed around the room.

"That's supposing I was the actual killer." Elspeth inspected her neon pink nails. "Of course, I would never have left the body or witnesses around to be discovered."

Groaning, Zach dropped into a padded chair next to Xandie. "Can we please stop talking about bodies? I've only got a certain amount of time free, so why doesn't someone give me a list of jobs. I'm good with lists."

Poor baby. Xandie didn't know what was worse, Elspeth planning a wedding or featuring as the number one murder suspect. She rubbed her hands over her fiancé's shoulders, fingers digging deep, massaging the knots out of his muscles.

Felicity cleared her throat. After a nod from Elspeth, she flipped the wedding planner's book open and ran her finger down the list, rattling off jobs as she went. "The groom and his groomsmen need to work out the suits and coordinate with myself and the florist over choice of boutonnieres."

Lila interrupted. "Button whatsit?"

"The male half of the bridal party wear flowers pinned to their suits. Traditionally worn to ward off bad luck. Maybe we should all wear a few." Everyone in the room stared at Holly who shrugged. "Don't look so surprised. I know a lot of things. I'm an enigma."

"Keep telling yourself that." Elspeth snapped her fingers at her assistant.

Felicity continued, "The dessert café hasn't answered my calls, so I need someone to pop in there and make sure they're ready to go with your confirmed cake choice. Also, the church hasn't contacted me either, so we need them to confirm." She looked expectantly at the cousins.

Sighing, Xandie stopped Zach's massage and held up a hand. So much for a quiet day working in her Library. "I'll speak to the girls about the cake and deal with the church. I just need a ride."

"Oh. Oh. Oh." Holly waved her hand wildly over her head. "I can do that."

"Enjoy the silver moped of boring death," Lila muttered.

"Hey." Holly glared. "Just because I observe the road rules doesn't make me boring.

"You don't stick to the speed limit. You do at least twenty under. You're a speed killjoy."

"At least I'm safe. Unlike that neon deathtrap of a van, my moped is very safe."

"Don't mock the van. It will eat your go-slow moped."

"Time out." Xandie held her hands up in a classic t-sign. "I just need a ride to Sinful Desserts and then the church. That's all. As long as I get there safely, without finding a dead body, I don't care who drives me."

Holly jumped up, grabbing her black helmet and plopping it on her head. She mumbled something unintelligible.

Sighing, Lila grabbed the visor and shoved it up. "How many times do we have to tell you, we can't hear you when you have your helmet visor down."

"I said, I'll show you speed killjoy. Crack on, Librarian. We have a timetable to get ahead of."

"See? That's the type of attitude we need." Elspeth beamed and clapped her hands. "On my mark...*go*."

"Elspeth, if I could have a few words..." Zach stood up and took a step forward.

"On that note, I'm gone." Xandie grabbed Holly and dragged her out of the Library. She loved her fiancé, but no way was she staying for an Elspeth interrogation. She'd rather deal with the moped boredom.

<hr>

"See. I told you I'm not a speed killjoy." Holly beamed as she placed her helmet on the moped parked in front of Sinful Desserts.

"Yep. This time, you were only ten under the speed limit. Kicking the traces, cuz." Xandie gave her cousin the thumbs up. Poor Holly. She wasn't exactly a rebel without a cause, but she did try in her own banshee way to live up to the Harrow name. And frankly, with no banshee visions and not even a hint of someone's impending death lately, Xandie was starting to wonder if Holly's banshee gifts were on the fritz.

"Ha. Wait until I tell Lila," Holly crowed.

"You do that, speed demon." Xandie handed Holly her spare helmet. "Let's get the cake stuff finished and get to the church before anything else goes wrong."

"Psst, Xandie. Over here." Ruby poked her head out from the alley that hugged the side of the shop. She motioned for the girls to join her.

"Is there a reason you're hiding outside?"

"Unfortunately." Ruby drew the women into the alley

and blew out a gusty breath. "There's an issue inside."

"Please don't tell me there's another dead body." Xandie bit her lip. She was starting to believe her wedding might just be jinxed.

"Worse. It's the health inspector. Your fiancé notified them of the death, and now they're conducting a surprise health inspection." Ruby rubbed her hands. "There's nothing to worry about, though. Our business follows every regulation. It was just a freak murder. No issues." Ruby looked at Xandie with plaintive eyes.

"Of course." Xandie faked a smile and patted the Devlin sister on the back. "Do you know anything more about Noelle's death?"

"That's the other reason I grabbed you. We heard the inspector talking to his head office. Apparently, peanut oil was added to our mix. It's not in the recipe. It was added afterward. They didn't even find the oil in our kitchen."

"Someone snuck in and added it. Were you guys both out of the kitchen at any time?"

Ruby shook her head at Xandie's question. "No. Never." She grimaced. "Actually, yes. I helped Lara set up the table for your cake testing. But I was only gone for five minutes, I swear."

"Five minutes is all the killer needed." Maybe Elspeth had a point. How far would Edgar go to get back at his sister and disrupt a Harrow-planned event?

"Look, I need to get back in there before the inspector realizes I'm gone. We'll keep you updated." Ruby flashed Xandie a brave smile. "I'm sure there'll be no more issues. Don't worry about anything. We have your reception and wedding cakes' back."

"Thanks, Ruby." At least something was going right. *Next stop, the church...*

EIGHT

"There's no such thing as a wedding jinx. Ruby said they didn't put the peanut oil in the cake. There's no reason to think the church will have any issues."

"Of course. You're right. I'm letting Elspeth and her shenanigans get to me." Xandie breathed in and out rhythmically, mentally counting down from ten in her head.

"Just let it go."

"If you start singing to me, I'm throwing down."

"That Theo's job. He's obsessed with karaoke."

Xandie opened her mouth to reply but was cut off by a high-pitched scream. Without thinking, she bolted up the church stairs and burst through the door, only to come to a shuddering halt.

"That's something you don't see very often." Holly pulled up next to her cousin. "I mean, how often do you see a reverend perched on a bucket screeching like an opera singer?"

This was Point Muse. Odds were, it wouldn't be the last time. "Reverend Harris? Is there an issue?"

"It's a plague." The reverend pointed a trembling finger

at the row of rats, line dancing through the middle of the church aisle.

"Rats." Squeaking, Holly backed away. "You're on your own, cousin. I have no time to go down with the bubonic plague this week." Holly turned tail and bolted out of the church.

"She's not just a speed killjoy but a scaredy cat banshee as well." Xandie winced as a group of rats peeled off the main line dancing group and ringed the frantic reverend who screeched again. "I'm sure we can get rid of the rats. Why don't you just step down from your bucket?"

"No. No. No." He shook his normally tidy gray head and his hair stood straight up. "I'm sorry. But the church must close immediately to deal with this infestation. Your wedding's cancelled."

And there it was... Harrow bad luck rearing its head. "An exterminator can deal with your rat issue. There's no need to be hasty about cancelling any events."

"I'm sorry, Alexandra. It isn't just about the rodents. We also have a nail fungus infestation. I was going to call you today anyway but was blindsided by the disease-ridden plague hounding me."

It was time to accept her fate. Her wedding was cancelled. "I'll let Elspeth know."

"Rodents are malicious when they decide to attack." Reverend Harris cleared his throat. "Ah, could you help..." He trailed off and gestured at the rats.

Xandie kicked a clear road out of the church for the terrified man.

Taking advantage, the reverend jumped off his bucket and raced down the aisle, joining Holly outside the church.

One of the rats spun to face the open door. It looked back at Xandie for a few seconds, and she'd swear it winked at her. Maybe the reverend was right about the malicious side of rats.

Backing up, Xandie took measured, slow steps toward the door.

As one, the rats formed into rows and stared unblinking at Xandie. A bride shouldn't have to deal with evil, line dancing rodents. Following the reverend's lead, Xandie bolted for the door, slamming it behind her. She rested against it, chest heaving.

Holly and the reverend stared, open mouthed, at Xandie.

A series of loud thumps sounded against the door.

"I think cancelling the wedding is a good idea, and maybe you should get two exterminators. Just in case." Xandie eased away from the door and scooted to the moped. "Good luck, Rev." Waving at the shocked man, Xandie slapped the moped's seat. "Come on, speed demon. We need to update Elspeth."

"Uh-huh." Holly clambered onto her moped and revved the engine before taking off at a speed foreign to the banshee.

Xandie made a note to mention to Lila that evil, line dancing rats were all the motivation the banshee needed to speed.

"I will hex that man, so his drawers fall down on Sunday."

"He can't help evil, line-dancing rats and a nail fungus infestation. It's the wedding. It's jinxed. Maybe we *should* just elope." Xandie demolished her hot chocolate in one long gulp. Rich, dark sweetness hit her tastebuds. She closed her eyes for a moment, blocking out Elspeth's meltdown.

"Are you listening to me, granddaughter?"

"Which one? Technically, you have three," Holly pointed out helpfully.

"You're not getting married and presenting me with possible future great grandchildren." Elspeth glared at the banshee. "Go and play with dead things. The adults are planning wedding retribution."

"We don't play with dead people. We prepare them. Got it? Prepare." Holly poked her tongue out at her grandmother.

"Man, you have a death wish. Plus, who knows where that tongue has been. Put it away. Health and safety." Lila whacked her cousin on the back of her head as she sat down at the table.

"Where's my assistant? Surely that mouthy wedding planner had backup plans for the wedding location?" Elspeth paced to and fro in front of the old stone hearth. The bakery was pretty much empty. Even the buzz-cut guy had disappeared.

"I think she took a call out back. I'll fetch her." Xandie jumped up before anyone could speak and made a beeline for the kitchen. Anything for a few seconds of peace. The kitchen stood empty, no wedding planning assistants in sight. Maybe Felicity had headed outside to the alley, away from nosy Elspeth's ears. Xandie spotted the door slightly ajar. The low murmur of Felicity's voice trickled through the small open gap.

"You know I'd do anything for you. Just let me deal with it."

Felicity must be seeing someone. The little half-brownie had kept that relationship very quiet.

"I have everything handled."

Xandie shuffled forward, scuffing her feet.

The assistant spun and quickly ended the call, stowing her phone away. "Ms. Meyers. Please don't tell Elspeth I was on a personal call. She's very focused on the wedding planning and wouldn't be impressed."

Someone deserved to have a little fun in their life. "I might be getting married now, but I still remember what it was like to have a secret romance. I won't breathe a word." Xandie wondered who the secret lover was.

Blushing bright red, Felicity dropped her head and mumbled her thanks as she passed Xandie. "I'd better get back in there before we have another issue."

"I think the next issue has already hit us. The church has a plague of rats and has cancelled the wedding."

Felicity nodded, seemingly unsurprised. "You'd be shocked how often that happens. I'll check the book. Noelle always had a plan B." She hustled out of the kitchen, Xandie following in her wake.

"And another thing. Those rats better be looking over their shoulders. One whisker out of place and I'll obliterate them. This is war."

Scurrying over to the wedding bible, Felicity started flicking through the pages.

Elspeth pointed at Xandie. "Do you believe now? Edgar's after my wedding. This is proof."

"I was under the impression it was Xandie's wedding. Didn't you have one of your own in the dark ages?"

"Be careful, baker girl. Your snark is showing, and you know what we do when that happens." Elspeth made snipping motions with her fingers.

"Can we not mention snipping. It gives me a complex,

doll face." Colin backed under a table, his voice echoing from underneath. "Wake me when the food's flying."

"Something will be flying soon if we don't calm the wicked witch down," Xandie muttered.

"Found it." Felicity held the book up to Elspeth. "Mayweather Inn has an ornate rose garden that would be perfect for a garden wedding. It's written in here as plan B. I'll give the owner a call and see if she has an availability."

"Oh, Rose will have an availability if she knows what's good for her." Elspeth bared her teeth. "This is all Edgar's fault. He's behind all of our issues." Elspeth's attention dropped away from Felicity and laser focused on something outside the bakery window. "And it's about time I let him know that..." Gathering her shadows around her like an old-fashioned petticoated skirt, Elspeth stomped out of the bakery onto Main Street. "You," Elspeth growled and stepped into the path of Edgar and his girlfriend.

"Me," Edgar agreed. "Do you have a counteroffer? A date for moving day?"

"I've got something for you all right. You wedding hater." Elspeth held up a lilac water balloon. "How about talking like a duck, burping bubbles, or a pulsating, blistering rash?"

Edgar reared back. "I am *not* a wedding hater. And such malicious accusation proves I'm the better Harrow. The house would benefit from my guidance."

"Guidance? From a dirty wedding saboteur? Messing with your own great-niece. I'm ashamed you're a Harrow," Elspeth shot back, chin poking out, fire in her eyes.

Xandie stepped up to the warring duo, standing next to Edgar's girlfriend, who was clothed in another floating chiffon, lemon-colored tea-dress. "I'm sure all the problems we're having with my wedding planning are just a coincidence."

"Ha," Elspeth scoffed. "The Harrow wastrel wanders back into town and immediately we start having issues with the wedding? Don't be so gullible, Library girl. You'll end up choking on all that innocence."

"Now, now. Why don't we all take a step back." Gigi beamed. "This is just a mix-up. A miscommunication. Besides, Edgar is a sweetie and loves weddings. After all, we *are* getting married ourselves." She flashed a large rock on her finger.

Elspeth rolled her eyes. "La-de-da. Bully for you and your sweetie. But if I catch either one of you interfering in the wedding, I'll go Armageddon on your skanky behinds."

Gigi gasped and stepped behind Edgar, holding onto the back of his jacket. "Goodness me."

"Typical. Just like our parents. You resort to threats. Aren't you a chip off the solid, unmoving block?" Edgar sneered.

"Why don't we all stop and think about what we're saying." Xandie took a small step forward, easing between Elspeth and her brother. Preventing all-out Harrow war in the middle of Main Street had just become her top priority.

"I don't need to calm down." Elspeth raised her hexed balloon high. "Unless you want to start speaking gobbledygook, clear the way, granddaughter."

"Bring it, you senile old witch." Edgar moved Gigi farther back and brought his hands up in a classic pugilist's stance. "I can take whatever hexes you throw my way. I *am* a Harrow after all. And for your information, we have nothing to do with any wedding issues you're having."

"Lies," Elspeth bellowed at her brother.

"Mother, we have other issues we need to deal with."

Winifred rushed up, her cheeks bright red. "You don't have time for family squabbles." Winnie grabbed her mother's arm and dragged her to the bakery entrance, whispering in her ear.

Spinning away from her daughter, Elspeth hid her hexed balloon back in her velour jogging-suit pants. "You're lucky, little brother, that there are other things on my mind right now." Sniffing, she stomped back inside the bakery.

"Definitely lucky. Oh my gosh. So lucky." Gigi tugged on Edgar's arm. "Let's go back to the inn, dearest. I think I need a drink after that."

"Don't we all," Xandie muttered as she watched her great uncle allow himself to be towed away. She turned to her aunt who still stood outside the bakery. "Is there really an issue?"

"I'm afraid so."

As long as the problem didn't include another dead body, Xandie could handle anything...*hopefully*.

NINE

"I'm cutting you off, Elspeth. No more." The tall, angular woman with straight, long, black hair made a slashing motion across her throat.

"I'll decide when we're done." Elspeth stood toe to toe with the other woman.

"Not when I get threatening letters. Dressmaking isn't worth losing my shop...or worse."

The woman flapped a torn piece of paper in front of Elspeth. "It's the first time I've ever had threats over a wedding dress. Pageant and prom, absolutely, but weddings?" The woman shook her head. "I'm done. Seriously."

She slapped the paper at Elspeth and stepped back, crossing her arms over her chest.

Xandie stepped up and grabbed the paper, scanning it. "Pay the price when you deliver the wedding dress. Sew at your own risk."

Since the only wedding dress the dressmaker currently sewed was hers, the implication was obvious. "Someone doesn't want me to have a wedding dress."

"I think that's an understatement." The woman waved her hand at a silk and lace concoction hanging on a dressmaker's dummy. "And it's not finished yet. I was going to get you in for a last-minute fitting this afternoon. Now I'm not sure it's in my best interest to even be seen talking to you."

"You'll do more than talk, Deborah Ann. You know what I'll do to you if you don't." Elspeth beamed, her dentures glittering in the light like sparkly shark teeth.

"Mother." Winifred sighed, exasperated. "I'm sure we can work around this."

"Do you Harrows ever take no for an answer?" The dressmaker flung her arms up and paced in front of Xandie's wedding dress.

"Not often. Way too stubborn," Xandie admitted. Sometimes that stubbornness led to bodies and the odd kidnapping or two.

"Well, I can be just as stubborn." Deborah Ann jutted out her jaw, unwilling to give in without a fight.

Elspeth inspected the interior of the dress shop. She tapped a painted nail on her chin. Little arcs of electricity escaped the nail, feathering her chin and neck. "You know, Deborah Ann? You've got a right to be worried. The shop is so fragile." Elspeth knocked on the wall and shook her head. "A stiff wind could knock this wall down, and you know how imps are. They're a pernicious infestation once they're entrenched."

"You're threatening me? Over a wedding dress?"

"Me? I'm just here to offer you a deal of a lifetime."

"Why do I think this deal has a catch?"

The poor dressmaker didn't sound so sure and neither did Xandie. The bewigged Point Muse witch was way too erratic to second-guess.

"How about I lay a nest of wards around your little

dress shop tomorrow? Lock it down tight. Nothing or no one with malicious intent will get in. Your business will be safe."

"What about me? What if someone targets me?"

"Here." Elspeth grabbed a baby pink ball and threw it at Deborah Ann. "Take this. Make sure you keep it in your pocket. Anyone comes up that you don't like, throw this at them. They'll end up plastered against the nearest solid object in pink goo."

Deborah Ann stared at the ball before switching her gaze back to Elspeth. "Why can't you layer the wards over my shop right now?"

"That's not how it works, Deborah Ann. Work first, then payment. As soon as you deliver my wedding dress and the bridesmaids' dresses, I will be here lickety-split, laying the wards. And I'll update them every year for four years. That's my best deal."

"I'll take it." The dressmaker held out her hand and Elspeth shook it.

"Ah, *my* wedding dress. Not yours, Elspeth. My wedding, remember?"

"What *evs*." Elspeth mouthed bridezilla at the dressmaker.

Clearing her throat, Deborah Ann gestured at the dress. "While you're here, we can do your final fitting. The sooner I get this dress done and out of my shop, the sooner Elspeth can ward the store."

Clapping her hands, Elspeth twirled on the spot. "Crack on, my girls. I've got nothing planned this afternoon. Bring on the fashion show."

"Speak for yourself. I've got a date with pizza and bridesmaid bonding." And possibly some tasty chocolate cocktails if Xandie had any say in it. Carbs, gossip, and at least five minutes of mayhem-free peace was all she required.

"You're a future serial killer. Because only someone psychotic likes pineapple pizza." Lila picked out a chunk of pineapple and pegged it at Holly, who snatched it out of the air and swallowed it.

"Tasty." Holly cackled, reminiscent of her grandmother. "Bring all your pineapple offerings to me, and I will grant you fruit-free pizza. This is my word."

"Freaky much?" Lila snarked back but dumped a handful of pineapple on her cousin's plate.

"Is this where we now have a heated debate about the pros and cons of fruit on a pizza?" Melody, Zach's younger sister and one of Xandie's bridesmaids, raised an eyebrow. "Because if the argument gets heated, I do have access to handcuffs."

Xandie guzzled a mouthful of her hot chocolate cocktail. "Frankly, I'm way too mellow to argue about the merits of fruit on pizza."

"That's the vodka and chocolate talking. Feel more relaxed now?"

"Thanks to you, Lila. This cocktail is amazing." Xandie toasted her cousin with her almost empty glass.

Snickering, Lila shoved a plate with a slice of pineapple-free pizza at her. "I think you'd better eat before I give you another drink."

"It's so good."

"Vodka, milk, chocolate, cocoa, bay leaf, and cloves. I'm calling it a hot chocolate late-night toddy."

"I call it a Librarian's hangover." Colin rolled onto his

back on the carpet. "I've got an itch; can anyone spare a hand?"

"Fine." Xandie carefully placed her drink on the coffee table next to her pizza. She dropped a hand to Colin's tummy and gave it a brisk rub. "And I don't have a hangover."

"Not yet." Lila pointed at the pizza. "Eat up or suffer in the morning."

"Why is every Harrow born bossy?" Xandie whined but complied, taking a large bite of the homemade pizza. "Oh, this is good, Lila. Really good."

"I'm thinking of offering savory pizza at the bakery. You three are my guinea pigs."

"Four." Colin rolled back onto his front with his mouth open, panting. "Feed me. Feed me. Feed me," he chanted.

"For Hecate's sake. How does Elspeth stand the complaining?" Lila slapped a slice on a paper plate and dumped it next to the hangry pug. "Don't even think about trying the chocolate cocktail either. We'll never hear the end of it from Elspeth."

Melody held up her amber-colored cocktail. "Or my honey cocktail. Trust me, this is amazing."

Xandie swallowed her mouthful of pizza. "Why are you here anyway, Colin? You're normally attached to Elspeth like a demonic parasite."

"That's my idea." Miranda stood in the open apartment door a moment before strolling in.

"Why would you inflict the always hungry black hole of a stomach on us? And why are you wearing all-black?" Xandie took another large bite of pizza, humming to herself as the tangy, savory flavors of meat lover's pizza sans pineapple hit her tastebuds.

"Hey. I resemble that remark." Colin snickered at his own joke before diving into the pizza.

"Because Nash and Matthew are out with your fiancé and his groomsmen. I thought it might be an idea to have someone who isn't drinking keep an eye out."

How weird was it that her mother's logic about the talking pug security system actually made sense to her? "And the black ninja outfit?" Her slim, muscled mother really did look menacing in black.

"Security patrol. Just making sure everything stays peaceful." Miranda scratched the back of her neck. "Just have the feeling that something's looming, so we'd better be prepared rather than be caught short."

Lila patted the lumpy couch next to her. "Sit and have pizza. We already thoughtfully removed the toxic pineapple."

"Hey. Pineapple is delicious." Holly grabbed another slice and loaded pineapple pieces on top.

"And that's why you work in a funeral home. You have a death wish. That and no taste."

Miranda accepted a slice of pizza and chewed, staring out Lila's apartment window.

"Penny for your thoughts, Mom?"

"I've seen that young man lurking around town again. He's definitely focused on Elspeth's brother, and he has skills. He's lying low currently but be wary of him."

Lila snorted. "Please. We'll do what we normally do."

"Wait until something happens and then send the big guns in to clear up the mess?" Holly poked a now dosing Colin with her toe.

"Don't forget your father arrived today. He's staying at the inn. Make sure you drop in and see him."

Xandie sighed. Her dad hated Point Muse, and

anything connected to the paranormal. And he definitely wasn't a fan of the Harrows either...except for her mother. His aunt Sera had been the Librarian to the Great Library before Xandie. And it made her dad hate the weird stuff even more. "I'll try. I just have to find time when Elspeth isn't around. You know how those two are together."

"Painful," Miranda agreed and stood, stretching. "Don't drink too much. You all need your wits about you to get through the next few days. Not to mention getting through the wedding and finding a killer." Miranda glanced out the window again, then frowned.

"What's wrong, Mom?" When an ex-black ops agent frowned, everyone should start getting worried.

"Your dressmaker's shop is just up from Sinful Desserts, correct?"

The three girls nodded.

"Do you know if the dressmaker's pulling an all-nighter?"

"No. After the last fitting, she finished up all the alterations. We're picking up my wedding dress first thing tomorrow morning. Why?" *Please, don't say it. Please, don't say it*, Xandie chanted mentally. She really didn't want anything else going wrong right now.

"Someone with a flashlight is in the shop."

And there it is...something else going wrong.

TEN

"Are you sure we don't need Great-Aunt Rose's finger for this? I don't think I should be arrested for breaking and entering by my fiancé a few days before our wedding."

"It's not breaking if someone has already entered." Miranda pointed at the partially open back door. "Someone did the hard work already."

"Speaking of hard work, I'm volunteering for lookout. I'm happy to sacrifice myself to help my cousin out."

"Suck it up, buttercup. We're all going in." Lila patted Holly on the back and gave Xandie a thumbs up.

"Here we go." Pushing open the door, Miranda slipped in, motioning for the others to follow. Xandie's mother flicked on her flashlight and ran it over the interior of the shop.

"Doesn't that ruin our element of surprise?" Holly whispered.

"The intruders are already gone. They achieved their mission," Miranda replied grimly and aimed her flashlight to where Xandie's dress hung in tatters.

"No," Xandie wailed and pushed her cousin aside

80

before lunging at her destroyed wedding dress. It hung off the dressmaker's dummy in strips. Someone had taken a knife and sliced the dress into silk and lace streamers. "Who could be so evil? So heinous as to destroy a wedding dress? Who?" Xandie wailed again and hugged the remnants of her dress.

"They were pretty thorough." Holly held up a pastel pink bridesmaid dress that now had large holes slashed into it.

"Maybe the slasher was a fashion critic." Lila pointed to her dress that had its puffy sleeves sheared off and a split sliced from breast down to the hem. "I mean, no offence, but those sleeves were nasty."

"You said you loved it." Xandie glared at her cousin.

"I lied. It's a rite of passage to wear crappy bridesmaid dresses. Who am I to spoil that for you?"

Holly nodded. "We've talked about it. We're fine with bridesmaid puffy horror dresses. We figured we'll get our own back when it's our turn."

"You hate my bridesmaid dresses?" Xandie pouted. Admittedly, she had paid more attention to her own dress and let Elspeth go to town on the bridesmaids' attire. In retrospect, that may have been a mistake.

"Hate's such a strong word."

Lila cut across Holly's words. "Yes. We hate them. But revenge, Harrow style, is sweet."

"You don't have to worry about it now, do you?" Xandie growled and held up a handful of her dress. "Look at this travesty. A crime against weddings." She glanced around the shop. "Not many places to hide. I take it the cowards have already bolted?"

Miranda prowled around the shop. "Looks like it. Unfortunately, sweetie, you're going to have to report this to your police chief. He needs to get his crime scene brownies down here as soon as possible. There might be something they can pick up. Some clue."

Xandie huffed and dropped her dress back onto the dummy. "I suppose. Have a poke around and see if the dress desecrater left any clues behind. I'll head out back to call. Better reception out there."

"Mother might be able to do something with your dress." Miranda rubbed her daughter's back as Xandie paused on her way past.

"With the way my luck's going, the dress will probably set Harrow House on fire," she muttered as she headed to the alley behind the shop. "Seriously, my wedding karma is definitely hinky."

A shuffling noise behind her was all the warning Xandie had before something crashed down hard on the back of her head. Blinding pain and tunnel vision forced her to her knees. *"Who..."* Xandie tried to force out words, but her tongue took up too much room for them to flow. Blackness crept in from the sides of her vision, smothering her. As she collapsed all the way to the ground, Xandie pushed out a hand and grabbed someone's leg as they moved in closer. A slim, muscled leg.

"Oi." A loud, gruff voice echoed through the alleyway.

Her attacker's muscles clenched under her hand before ripping away from her grip. The sound of shoes slapping against cobblestones decreased in volume as the noise blended with the normal Point Muse night.

"Crap." The gruff voice that scared her attacker off sounded next to Xandie as she fought to stay conscious. "You'll be okay. Hang on, I need to check your head."

Gentle hands probed the back of Xandie's head. She hissed as her rescuer's fingers drew too close to her wound.

"Bit of a cut but not too bad. You're going to have a heck of a headache though." Her rescuer carefully laid Xandie's head back on the ground. "I'll make sure your family finds you, but I can't get caught here. Not yet."

Blackness slunk into her consciousness like a shadowy stalker as two large bangs of the dressmaker's back door heralded her family's arrival.

"Xandie's down. Call the healers and Braun." Miranda knelt next to her daughter. "Alexandra? Can you hear me, sweetie? You need to stay awake until the healers get here."

Xandie forced words past her dry, swollen tongue. "Man. Here."

"No one's here." Lila crouched next to Xandie as Holly spoke rapidly into a phone.

"Man save me. Other hit my head."

"It's okay. We'll sort this out. You stay still." Miranda soothed her daughter as flashing lights lit the dark alley and sirens blared.

Braun rushed into the alley with a healer on his heels. He knelt next to his fiancée. "If you really wanted to elope, all you needed to do was tell me."

"Not. Funny." Xandie pushed herself partially up on her elbows, and a white heat exploded through her skull, fading everything, including her not-so-funny fiancé, to black nothingness. Peace at last.

***

"There." Winifred placed a steaming mug of hot tea next to Xandie and plumped up the cushions on the couch she reclined on. "A hot, sweet tea is good for shock and for cleansing the soul."

"Hey, where's my tea? Maybe a cake or two? I want the

Winnie special as well," Colin whined. "Maybe I need to fall on my head too."

"It wouldn't help." Lila rolled her eyes and pointed at the mouthy pug. "She got attacked. She didn't fall on her head. Although Aunt Winnie's pampering this morning is a tad over the top. Xandie has legs and can walk to the kitchen for her own tea. The healers worked on her head last night. She's fine."

"Et tu, Brutus?" Xandie took a small sip of tea and sighed as the liquid gold warmed her insides.

"Just telling it like it is."

"Speaking of telling us, I can't wait any longer. What happened last night?" Winifred clasped her hands together, knuckles white.

Xandie carefully placed her tea on the small table next to her couch. Harrow House helpfully scooted the table closer, so she didn't have to reach so far. "Thanks, House." She patted the table. A sentient house filled with the remnants of Harrow magic was definitely helpful sometimes. "We saw lights in the dressmaker's shop and decided to investigate. Found my dress and the bridesmaids' dresses sliced up. I went out to the alley to call Zach, and someone whacked me on the head."

"Did you see anyone?" Holly bit her lip. "Maybe the ghost of the wedding planner took you out?"

"Not unless the ghost works out. I grabbed someone's leg when I hit the ground. It felt muscular. Muscled but skinny, if that makes sense."

"Complete sense. A skinny, muscular ghost with wedding envy tried to take you out." Holly nodded. "We need to get crosses to protect ourselves."

"Calm down, Van Helsing. And crosses are for vampires, not ghosts. I'm also pretty sure ghosts don't work out." Lila leaned forward and encouraged Xandie. "What else do you remember?"

My rescuer. "Someone yelled out. Scared whoever it was who hit me. I heard them running in the opposite direction."

"Did you see your helpful rescuer?" Lila tapped her fingers on her knee. "Or sense anything about them? Male? Female?"

"I was pretty much out of it. But it was a man. He told me I'd be okay. That he'd make sure my family found me. But he couldn't get caught. *Not yet.* Sounded like he had something to do. He did sound familiar, but I've got no clue where I've heard his voice before." Xandie carefully rubbed the back of her head.

"Stop whining. The healers removed the injury last night, and you still have your brains today. I take that as a win." Elspeth stomped into the sitting room with Felicity following behind her, her precious wedding bible cradled in her arms.

"Hey, I still have a headache." Xandie sat up and glared at her grandmother. "And I don't have a wedding dress. I'm entitled to be upset."

"Just call me your fairy godmother." Elspeth fluffed her blonde, Farrah Fawcett-style, blow-waved wig and snapped her fingers.

Felicity placed the bible on a coffee table and scuttled back out before returning with a dress she carefully laid along the top of the couch.

"Since when are you a fairy godmother? You're always the wicked witch in our Harrow stories." Lila narrowed her eyes. "What do you have planned?"

"For Hecate's sake." Elspeth stomped over to the dress. She held up a cream-colored wedding dress. "There's your wedding dress. But you'd better make sure it comes back to me in the same condition."

"It's beautiful." Xandie eased out of her seat, drawn toward the dress. "You didn't knock someone off for it, did you?" She fingered the lace of the tiny see-through sleeves that gathered at the shoulder.

"It's my wedding dress." Elspeth smoothed a hand over the sweetheart neckline. "I looked like a goddess in it. Probably still fits me."

Lila, Holly, and Winifred crowded in next to Xandie.

"It's beautiful, Elspeth. You sure I can use it?"

"Well, it's the only wedding dress we have. I threw your mother's hippy dress out because of all the stains."

"Food. Food stains." Winifred blushed bright red.

Elspeth snorted. "All the herbs floating around on that day, I'm surprised you can remember anything." She shoved the dress at Xandie. "You should see if it fits."

Xandie carefully took the dress and held it up against her. "It might actually fit me." The creamy silk dress had a sweetheart neckline, gathered short sleeves, and a fitted bodice that led into a flowing skirt with delicate lines of beading down it.

"My mother loved sewing and collected the beads and lace from her mother and grandmother. It wasn't normal to have a lot of beading or embroidery during that time. She wanted me to have some of my Harrow ancestors with me on my wedding day."

"That's so sweet. Especially for a Harrow." Holly sniffed and wiped her moist eyes. "I must have a cold. Maybe allergies."

"Yeah. That's what it is, banshee," Lila gently mocked her cousin.

A loud banging filled the room, and Elspeth's wedding dress spell broke.

Winifred grimaced. "If the House isn't letting our visitor in, they're probably more foe than friend."

Lila moved to the window and peeped out. "I wouldn't count on it. I think the House has decided your fiancé shouldn't see the wedding dress yet."

"Zach?" Xandie carefully draped the dress back on the couch and raced to the window. She pushed it open and stuck her head out. "The House doesn't want to let you in."

Zach sauntered across the porch to Xandie's open window. "Have I upset it?"

"Not yet." Xandie winked. Harrow House loved the bear shifter in an almost girlish fashion. The door was always open to him and lights inside the house always emitted a rosy gleam when he turned up to visit. "I was looking at a wedding dress, and I don't think the House wanted you to see it."

"You found a replacement one already?"

"Elspeth's wedding dress. It's gorgeous."

"Uh-huh." The bear shifter arched an eyebrow. "And your grandmother just happened to have one laying around for you to use?"

"That's right, bear boy. I'm just helpful like that." Elspeth poked her head up over the top of Xandie's. "Why are we being afflicted with your presence this morning?"

Ignoring Elspeth, Zach turned to Xandie. "Matthew and I are heading up to Portland to pick up the suits. I just wanted to let you know. In case you needed to get hold of me."

"Oh, that's sweet." Holly poked her head out from the other side of Xandie.

"Seriously? In person? You could have called her." Lila crowded in next to Xandie.

"You know, I never realized how big these windows were before."

"That's why I don't live in Harrow house. No privacy." Xandie wiggled and pushed her cousins and grandmother back. "Are you sure you want to marry into this family?"

"I prefer to think of it as you marrying into mine." Zach leaned forward and tweaked Xandie's nose before brushing a light kiss across the top of it. "Try not to find another dead body or break into someone else's shop while I'm out of town. I don't want to miss all the drama."

"I hate sarcasm." Xandie grabbed Zach's shirt and yanked him closer, pressing a heated kiss to his mouth. She pushed him away, snickering as his glazed eyes cleared. "Drive safely."

Zach saluted her and joined Matthew in the unmarked cruiser.

"Ew, bear cooties." Lila cackled.

"That killed the mood." Sighing, Xandie watched as the men reversed down the driveway. Because of all the drama with the wedding planner, she'd barely seen her fiancé except when she found a body, broke into a shop, or got attacked.

An expensive SUV cruised into the driveway and pulled to a stop. The passenger door swung open, and the lemon-yellow, stiletto-clad Gigi slid out. She stood up and held the door for balance.

"Yoo-hoo, Alexandra. Could you be a dear and come here? These new heels are murder on my feet."

It would be murder if Elspeth found her talking to Edgar's other half. Risking a glance over her shoulder, Xandie spotted Elspeth arguing with her cousins. Taking the initiative, Xandie clambered out of the open window. *It really is large.*

Slipping down the porch stairs, Xandie stood a few paces away. "What can I do for you, Gigi?"

"Edgar asked me to make sure you were okay after he heard about your accident."

"It wasn't an accident. Someone hit me over the head. *After* destroying my dress."

"How horrible." Gigi pressed a hand over her mouth, then let it drop. "And your wedding dress? Surely your wedding can't go ahead if you don't have a dress?"

"Don't bet on it," Xandie muttered. She pasted on a fake, insincere smile and shot it point-blank at Gigi. "Elspeth has offered her wedding dress. I guess we're all set. Aren't I lucky?"

Gigi's eyes widened. "So lucky." She shuddered. "No offense, but I'd never wear a second-hand dress. Too many issues."

Issues? "What kind of issues?" Did she mean stains? That's what dry-cleaning was for.

"Psychic imprints." Gigi nodded. "It's the biggest day of a bride's life. Good and bad. Some weddings don't end well. Vibrations and impressions cling. And wearing the wicked witch of Point Muse's wedding dress? You're very brave."

Great, now I can't get bad vibes and Elspeth's wedding dress out of my head. "Sorry to sound rude, but why are you here, Gigi?"

"My goodness. So direct." Gigi trilled a laugh. "As I said, just to check on you. My Edgar insisted. I don't like to say no to him." She forced a smile. "He can get a bit grumpy if you don't do what he asks. So much easier to go with the flow."

Was Gigi implying that Edgar had a temper? Or that

the Harrows should do what he said? "Elspeth has a temper too. Must be a Harrow trait."

"That must be it." Gigi changed the subject. "I just love weddings. As does Edgar. We're wedding groupies really."

"Angling for an invitation, Barbie?" Elspeth stood on the porch stairs, glaring at Edgar's fiancée.

"Elspeth, darling. So nice to see you. I was just having a fiancée-to-fiancée chat with Alexandra. We heard about her injury."

"Sympathetic and compassionate are not Edgar's middle names. What do you really want?"

"Elspeth," Xandie warned her grandmother. The wicked witch wasn't exactly sane when it came to her younger brother.

"No. No. It's understandable. I won't keep you any longer. I know you're deep in wedding plans. Ciao, sweetie." Gigi slipped back into her SUV, slamming the door shut.

Xandie backed up until she stood on the steps next to Elspeth. Both watched the car head down the drive until it disappeared.

"What did she really want?"

"To warn us about Edgar's temper and implying I shouldn't wear the dress because it could have bad vibes attached from your wedding day angst."

Elspeth snorted. "I wouldn't worry about wedding day angst sticking to the dress. I'd be more concerned with the stab wound and witch's curse on it."

"Yeah." Xandie whipped her head around and stared at her grandmother. "Wait. *What?*"

"Didn't I mention that?" Elspeth winked and sauntered back inside.

As a parting comment, that one was a zinger.

ELEVEN

"Why did I have to chauffer you and the great bridezilla down to the florist?" Lila opened the door to Point Muse's one and only flower shop and ushered her grandmother and Xandie inside.

"Not bridezilla. I'm the wedding planner. Can't you tell?" Elspeth smoothed her blonde wig with a bun coiled over each ear. "I even dressed appropriately."

Xandie fought not to stare at her grandmother, but the urge was just too strong. Elspeth had paired the blonde wig with a white camouflage, velour jogging suit and matching combat boots with a red stripe down the side. The wicked witch of Point Muse could blind with her sartorial brightness. "Why are you wearing white?"

"We all know you're more suited to black-on-black. Pure evil is allergic to bright white," Lila muttered.

"I heard that. I can always hex your underwear drawer shut. And now that your reaper boyfriend has moved in, it'd be his underwear drawer as well." Elspeth sniffed. "Felicity says white is a power color, and as the only wedding planner in town, I have to present a professional image."

"You're a wicked witch, not a wedding planner," Xandie replied automatically. "Speaking of Felicity, I thought she'd be here."

"Personal time. I think she's got a new beau. She wanted to sneak off and buy him a little keepsake. The way she was dancing around the subject, I gather it was some sort of paltry three-week anniversary or something sappy like that. Wasn't hard to read between the lines." Elspeth clapped her hands and bellowed, "Business is awaiting."

"Yeah. That's professional." Lila leaned against the counter. "Why are we here, anyway?"

"I'm just checking the wedding bouquets on order are okay." Xandie hesitated. All her cousins were sarcastic and loved to make fun of each other, but she had a nebulous feeling of bad things coming for her wedding. Lila would probably mock her for her feelings, but Xandie just wanted to make sure everything was going to plan, flower wise.

"Harrow bad feeling?"

"Maybe. You don't want to make fun of me?"

"Your Harrow bad luck-o-meter is more finetuned than mine. If you've got a funny feeling, I trust it." Lila wandered around the store, running a hand over the shelves. She showed her palm to Xandie. "I think your bad feeling was right on target. A dirty business is never a good sign."

"I don't disparage your place of work. Please don't criticize mine." A large woman with bright orange hair stepped out from the back office, where a curtained window faced the interior of the store. "What do you want, Elspeth?"

"Oh, not me. My favorite granddaughter wants to check on the status of her wedding order. I assured her there'd be no problems. Alley cat here is a top-notch professional florist." Elspeth turned to Xandie. "Didn't I say that?"

Nodding her head mechanically, Xandie swallowed.

She just knew something bad was about to slap her in the face like a wet fish going in for the kill.

"Alison. My name is Alison." The florist reached under her desk and drew out a shriveled and dead-looking, pastel-themed wedding bouquet. She slapped it on the counter, and tiny green bugs showered the grimy glass. "I was about to call you anyway."

Elspeth hissed and reared back, pointing at the sad looking bunch of very dead flowers. "What is that monstrosity?"

"Those are all aphids. Normally, they cause little damage to plants, but I've never seen them in such numbers. Large quantities can stop the growth of the plant and cause it to die. This is what I received from my supplier. This is *not* my fault." She crossed her arms. "The issue could've been handled by him before it got to this point. Now it's too late. I can't fulfill your order."

Xandie nodded. Right now, she was too numb to even react. It felt like Groundhog Day. Another day, another wedding issue. In a haze of denial, Xandie peered around the store. The bright red poppy curtains at the office window caught her attention. As did the shadowed figure showcased behind the curtain listening to every word spoken. "Did your employees source out any other supplies that might help us?"

Alison drew herself up. "I am the only employee, and I can assure you, I did my due diligence. No one can supply you in such a tight turnaround. I'm afraid that's the reality." Alison stomped out from behind the counter and held her door open. "Now, if you'll excuse me. I need to take inventory." She waited for the trio to exit before slamming the door shut and locking it.

"Friendly woman."

"Suspicious woman, you mean."

"Why suspicious?" Elspeth raised an eyebrow at Xandie.

Xandie turned away from the shop and answered her grandmother's question. "Because she has no other employees, but someone was in her office listening closely to our conversation."

Elspeth grinned, her predatory dentures on show. "Isn't it good then that I know her supplier? It's time for a road trip, ladies."

More ominous words were never spoken.

"What have I done to be cursed with your presence, Elspeth Harrow?" A short, skinny, older man with enormous gray, bushy eyebrows sat on his tractor glaring down at the wicked witch.

"You're just sore about losing that last hand of poker, Jasper. But I'm here to bring glad tidings." Elspeth beamed.

"For my sanity's sake, don't smile. Triggers my angina." He rubbed his chest. "Spit it out, card shark. What do you want?"

"To wipe out the debt you owe me."

"Elspeth's still stockpiling her poker debts?" Xandie whispered.

Lila nodded. "Like a rabid collector."

Jasper narrowed his gaze. "What's the catch?"

"We need information."

"Information, I can supply." Belying his gray hair, Jasper slipped off the tractor and strode toward his farmhouse porch. "Take a seat and tell me what you need."

"That orange-haired menace of a florist said you gave

her dead, bug infested flowers for my granddaughter's wedding bouquet. Say it ain't so, Jasper." Elspeth drummed her fingernails on the arm of the wooden chair. "I don't hate you yet. Don't make me change my mind."

The farmer slammed his hand down on a porch railing. "That lying besom. I sent her the best quality buds I had. Special for the Librarian."

He growled and paced on the porch. "If there's something wrong with the flowers, it isn't from my end."

"Aphids." Xandie joined the conversation. "She showed us the bouquet. It was full of aphids that apparently came from your farm."

"Lies," the farmer bellowed and shook his fist in the air. "I should have known better than to trust that shyster."

"Alison *is* a fat cat snake, but a shyster?" Elspeth leaned forward. "Tell me more, poker buddy."

Jasper gave up his pacing and slipped into a wooden porch chair. "That woman has a reputation for cutting corners. Anything for a quick buck or two. In fact,"—he lowered his voice—"I've heard a rumor she visits the black market regularly."

"There's a black market for flowers?" Lila shook her head. "Who knew?"

"I did. Now shut it." Elspeth pointed at Jasper. "Anything else?"

Reaching into a pocket, he drew out a business card and flicked it at the witch. "Some out-of-town lawyer came poking his nose into my stock. Wanted to buy up everything I had ready to ship."

Grabbing the card off Elspeth, Xandie read it out loud. "James Neville, lawyer. Moulton Street. Portland, Maine. That sounds suspiciously like Great-Uncle Edgar's lawyer."

"Edgar," Elspeth growled.

"Calm down until you're off my land. I've got vulnerable plants here. Think happy thoughts. Lucky for you, I've got some good news."

"You know who the killer of my wedding planner and the possible orchestrator of my wedding's demise is?" *It's worth a shot.*

"Nope. But I have more of the stock you want for your wedding. I can deliver it Harrow House, as long as you've got someone with skills to arrange it."

"Hot diggity, Jasper. Consider your debt cancelled. We'll get Winnie to have a crack at arranging. She's crafty and creative." Elspeth rubbed her hands together. "Right now, top of my list is another talk with our bouquet-killing florist."

"What kind of talk?" Lila asked.

"My kinda talk." Elspeth cackled, and something smashed inside the farmer's house.

"Dang it, woman. Quit the hag act, or I'll have no crystalware left," Jasper bellowed.

"I think the florist won't be interested in your talk anytime soon, or ever for that matter." Xandie winced as Elspeth nudged the florist's still body with the toe of a combat boot.

"That's what you get when you do a deal with a devil called Edgar."

"You seriously think your younger brother would kill a florist?" Lila prowled around the body and pointed out the wedding bouquet that lay next to the florist's hand. "I think he might be our culprit."

A gray rattlesnake with a pinkish stripe down his back curled around the base of the bouquet.

"A timber rattlesnake. Endangered and not native to Maine." Elspeth scooped up the snake, cooing to it. "Aren't you a pretty thing. You'll be perfect in the vivarium in my creation cave."

Xandie shuddered. "Firstly, aren't you worried it will bite you, and secondly, what's a vivarium?"

"She's too mean to get bitten, and it would kill the snake."

"I can hear you, Lila Harrow." Elspeth stroked the stripe down the snake's back. "A vivarium is a glass-fronted case like an aquarium, but for amphibians and reptiles. Like my pretty here."

"Okay. Thanks for the information download, and I'm never stepping foot in your cave ever."

"You were never invited, Lila, dear." Elspeth stepped over the corpse and continued to the door, stopping for a moment to issue instructions. "Best you let your dearest know we have another casualty in our wedding war."

Xandie grabbed her special Elspeth-spelled phone. "What wedding war?"

"The one I'm gonna win with extreme prejudice. Edgar Harrow's toast." Elspeth headed out to Main Street, the slam of the shop door heralding her exit.

"It's time to panic." Lila grabbed Xandie's arm tightly.

"I've been panicking all along. Why are you joining me now?"

"Elspeth mentioned war. Whenever that word appears in her vocabulary, it means maximum carnage and maximum mayhem, wicked witch style."

The urge to flee and avoid the upcoming catastrophe burned in Xandie's chest like an Elspeth-caused indigestion.

Could one take a honeymoon before getting married?

TWELVE

"Zach's giving us thirty minutes. In and out. He's left the door unlocked. We don't even have to use Great-Aunt Rose's skeleton key finger to get us in." Xandie pushed the florist's back door open. Her fiancé had *not* been impressed to find another body connected to their wedding but had agreed to them searching the florist shop...with a time limit applied.

"Did you bribe him with extra nooky time?"

"What's nooky time?"

Holly shrugged. "Couple stuff that I can't do because, you know...*single*."

"And likely to remain so if you keep calling it nooky time." Lila grimaced. "The word leaves a bad taste in my mouth."

"I bet Elspeth has a potion for that." Holly shuddered. "She has a potion for everything. Speaking of the wicked witch...where is she?"

"I don't know, which doesn't calm me. On the other hand, it allowed me to raid her hex bombs in case of trouble." Xandie patted her bulging pocket.

Lila whistled. "Planning this wedding has you walking on the wild side. Elspeth won't be impressed you meddled in her creation cave."

Nash, Lila's protective hellhound, growled low in his throat. "Run. Prey."

Xandie stared wide-eyed at the mouthy hound. "Did he call me prey and tell me to run?"

"Eh." Lila shrugged and rubbed her hellhound's slinky ears. "He knows Elspeth."

"Fair enough." Xandie pushed the florist's door wide open and issued her orders. "Put Nash on guard duty. Only those of Harrow blood or significant others who don't want to kill us can get in. Got it? We need to search the shop. We now have twenty-eight minutes and counting."

"You're sounding way too much like Elspeth lately."

Xandie glared at Holly. "That's the nastiest thing you've ever said to me. Now search."

"Such a slave driver," Holly whined and stomped to a far corner of the store, poking at dried bundles of flowers. "It's dead in here. *Literally*."

"Then you should feel at home, banshee."

"Just think of the germs decomposing flora could generate." Holly shivered and wiped her palms on her black jeans. "I'm rethinking my participation."

"Maybe you should rethink your preoccupation with germs."

Xandie pinched her nose. "Could you two please stop squabbling? We don't have time for this tonight."

"Please. We live for squabbling. We're Harrows." Lila poked her tongue out.

"Do what you want. I'm checking out the florist's office. Try not to kill each other. I've had enough of finding bodies lately." Xandie loved her cousins like sisters, but sometimes she wished Elspeth would hex them mute for a few minutes. She slipped into the small office, the curtains still drawn across the window that overlooked the shop. Xandie checked and could see the shadowed forms of her cousins. Someone had definitely been listening to them when they were there earlier. "Probably the killer." Muttering to herself, she poked through the correspondence on the desk. Mostly invoices and all overdue.

"Not exactly a booming business then." Xandie opened a mustard-colored, metal filing cabinet that had seen better days. "Most people are digital these days, but the florist had old school tendencies." She fished out a dark green ledger and flicked through it.

"Find anything?" Lila paused in the doorway. "Not exactly room for a party in here."

"She was short on space and capital." Xandie held up the ledger. "This says she was pretty much running on empty. Even the cash from our wedding wouldn't keep this shop afloat for another week."

"Why keep trading then? Not to mention sabotaging your wedding bouquets. She wouldn't get paid if she cancelled your order. So, why do it if she needed the cash?"

Dropping the ledger back into the filing cabinet, Xandie turned and scanned every nook and cranny of the office. It didn't take long. "Exactly. If you're desperate for cash, you wouldn't. But what if she wasn't that desperate because she knew she had a big payday coming?"

"Meaning she was paid to sabotage your flowers."

"I think she has a second accounting ledger for her dodgy dealings." Xandie scratched her nose in thought. "The killer might just be getting rid of loose ends or..."

"Or the florist tried to blackmail the killer."

Xandie winked. "It's like you've done this before."

"Just for once, it would be nice if it wasn't blackmail." Lila rolled up the sleeves of her dark-colored shirt. "What do you want me to do?"

"If you were a book of dodgy dealings, where would you hide?"

"Firstly, no Harrow would be so stupid as to have physical evidence of alleged wrongdoings. But if I wasn't a Harrow, I would want it close to me. Somewhere I can access it easily and keep it in sight."

"Exactly." Xandie ran a hand over the back of the filing cabinet and under the desk as well but couldn't find any false bottoms. "The notebook must be here, but the office is too small to have a secret room. Or a hidden alcove behind the bookcase."

Lila nibbled on her lip. "And not much room for anything else. The most she could do was sit at that old desk."

"You are such a smart cookie." Xandie beamed and ran her hand over the chair.

"Could you not mention cookies?" Lila fake gagged. "We all know cookie baking is my kryptonite."

"Aha." Xandie edged a hand down the untidy seam on the back of the chair. She slipped her fingers in and drew out a small black notebook, no bigger than her hand.

"She was literally sitting on the evidence."

Flipping through to the last notation, Xandie read it aloud. "Twenty thousand. Moulton Street, Portland. No name. Just a quick notation underneath to explore all future financial options."

"Blackmail." Lila winked. "It's always greed that gets them in the end."

"Moulton Street." Xandie tapped the notebook. *Where have I heard that street name before?*

"You look constipated. Do you need Elspeth's prune juice special?"

Xandie gagged. "No thanks. One upset stomach after tasting it was enough. No. I'm sure I've heard that street name before. Recently." She closed the notebook with a snap. "Lawyer's address on the business card that Elspeth's poker buddy, Jasper, gave us. That address was Moulton Street in Portland."

"I spy a road trip in our future."

"Um, guys?"

"We'll be out in a second. Cool your jets," Lila hollered.

"Nope. We have a problem that needs your attention." Holly's voice squeaked on the last word.

"This wedding is nothing but a problem. I'm having flashbacks when anyone mentions problems." Sighing, Xandie held onto the notebook but followed Lila. To find Holly in the middle of the store, keeping very still.

"Are we playing statues?" Lila poked her cousin in the rib cage.

Holly hissed and jerked her head at the back door. "I was told not to move."

"By whom?"

Grabbing hold of Lila, she turned her cousin around until she faced a dark shadow next to the back door. "By him."

A shadow detached from the wall and stood facing the girls. A black, hooded jumper covered the shadow's head.

"If you've hurt my dog, you're in for a world of Harrow hurt." Lila stepped in front of Holly, fists clenched.

"Your dog's fine. I gave him a tummy rub, and he let me in."

The three girls exchanged glances.

"My hellhound let you rub his stomach and then allowed you inside?"

"I would never hurt a guard dog for doing its job, or any animal, for that matter."

Xandie hid the hand that held the notebook behind her back and grasped for a hex bomb in her pocket with the other. "What do you want?"

"What you've got behind your back."

Curses! I'm not used to eagle-eyed villains. Normally, they were incompetent. Xandie held the book up. "What good is it to you?"

"That's my business. Hand it over. I really don't want to hurt anyone."

Villains never did, but it always happened anyway. Xandie threw the notebook over her shoulder. "Whoops. Seems like you need to come and get it. Why don't you tell us your name, by the way?"

"My name isn't important."

"Yeah, it is." In fact, there was something familiar about the hooded figure. Something about his voice Xandie needed to remember.

"Shouldn't we be *not* antagonizing him?" Holly hissed.

"Why? It's just some rando thief who's here as illegally as we are." Lila waggled a finger at the hooded man. "Breaking and entering. How naughty."

"It's not breaking and entering if the door's unlocked. It's just entering," the figure growled.

"That's what we say, but no one ever believes us." Holly nodded sagely. "I think it's because we're Harrows."

"I know you, don't I?" It was his voice. Pain suddenly gripped the back of her head for a moment, before releasing. Xandie rubbed the spot where her assailant had hit her.

That's it. "You scared off my attacker in the alley. You spoke to me. I recognize your voice."

"You always pay for the good deeds, they say." He heaved out his breath. "You didn't deserve to go out ambushed in a dirty alley like that."

"You saved me then, so why attack me now?"

"I need that book."

He seemed fixated on the florist's dirty ledger. But why? What did he expect to find in it? "I guess you need to come and get it then." Xandie gripped one of Elspeth's smoke bombs before sliding closer to her cousins.

"Do you really think I'm that stupid? That I don't research all the active players? You're always planning something." He held up a small, rainbow-colored, metallic ball. "So am I."

They both launched at the same time. The metallic ball and Elspeth's smoke hex met in the middle of the room with a concussive bang. Arrows of blue light speared through the shop, and smoke billowed out, covering the room in thick gray clouds.

Xandie yanked Lila and Holly to the ground, and as one, the trio shifted to the side of the room, backs against the wall.

"I'll find that book, Ms. Meyers. I never miss a target." The man's voice seemed to come from multiple areas of the room at once, and Xandie couldn't pinpoint where he stood. But her mysterious shadow man sounded like a military guy or a black ops agent, zeroing in on a target.

"Neither do I."

Her fiancé's low voice rumbled through the room, as did a blindingly bright spotlight that cut through the smoke, illuminating the trio of Harrows crouched near the wall and a hooded figure.

The police chief jerked his head at Xandie. "Time for another visit downtown, sweetie. You ladies know the drill." He angled the spotlight, so the hooded man's face showed clearly.

Buzz cut guy from the bakery was her alley rescuer and black book acquirer.

Why is he obsessed with Edgar Harrow?

THIRTEEN

"How come he gets bailed out after one little phone call, and I get disapproving parents?" Xandie crossed her arms and sulked from her perch on the corner of Melody's desk.

"I'm only disapproving that you got caught." Xandie's mother clucked her tongue. "Your grandmother would be so disappointed with your life choices."

"Elspeth Harrow doesn't make life choices. She reels from drama to drama, causing chaos and mayhem as she goes." Nicolas Meyers frowned at his daughter. His elegant brow beetled. "Trust me, you do *not* need to emulate that woman."

"Now, dear. Elspeth isn't that bad," Miranda soothed her husband.

Xandie arched an eyebrow at her mother's outlandish statement.

"All right. She *is* that bad. In fact, she's much worse than everyone thinks."

"I'm more worried about where she is currently. She normally never avoids the chance to rail away at the establishment, a.k.a. Big Brother, a.k.a. the cops." Xandie nibbled on the corner of her lip. An absent Elspeth boded ill for everyone in Point Muse. Just what was her wedding-crazed grandmother up to?

"She's probably checking her witch shine stills. We're raiding them tonight." Aggie strolled over and squeezed Xandie in a tight bearhug before letting her go. "How are you holding up, sweet pea?"

"This isn't the first time my fiancé's taken me in for questioning."

"And probably not the last either." Lila wandered out from the station's break room, munching on one of her own baked bear claws. "I must say I'm a brilliant baker. These are delicious."

"And so modest too," Xandie teased.

"If I can't toot my own horn, no one can. At least I stayed. Our germaphobe cousin ran away as soon as she finished being questioned. Something about catching the plague from sitting in the same seat as criminals."

Xandie snickered. Holly was always there to help her family, but she had a definite issue with germs.

Nicolas pinched the bridge of his nose. "Can we get back to the fact Elspeth's about to be raided by local law enforcement?"

Aggie snorted. "There's no raiding. We give her plenty of time to secure her operations. We'll get there after she's shifted the whole still operation. Win-win."

"How is tipping off the target of your raid a win-win situation?" Nicolas stared wide-eyed at Xandie's future mother-in-law.

"The person who rang in the complaint sees we're dealing with the issue, and we get to keep on living. Win-win."

"And Elspeth?"

"Elspeth has the hassle of moving her stills and setting up shop again. It's a process." Aggie shrugged. "Plus, she's ramped up her production because of the wedding. So, it'll be a massive undertaking to move everything. That's punishment enough."

"Of course. Why shouldn't we have witch shine at the wedding?" Nicolas threw up his hands and muttered under his breath.

Xandie winced. Her dad had a mental block when it came to Point Muse and the Harrows. The less time spent with either, the better as far as he was concerned. Xandie was amazed he'd even agreed to come to the wedding at all.

Her back-alley rescuer stepped out from the interview room and nodded to the police chief before heading outside. Xandie narrowed her gaze. Lines had furrowed his forehead, and his eyes were bloodshot. He gently rubbed them and winced. Just like her father did when he had contact lenses in. Did her rescuer have poor sight? Or was he hiding the color of his eyes for another reason? Making a snap decision, Xandie ignored her family and strolled outside, surprising her fellow police station escapee. "You might as well tell me your name. Since it's probably police record now. Besides, we all know you used an alias. At least I don't have to keep calling you my back-alley rescuer."

"Liam." He turned around and faced Xandie. "I'm glad you're okay. That was a nasty hit you took in the alley."

"Thanks to you, I am. And I might even make it to my wedding, if someone would stop sabotaging it." Xandie squinted. "Know anything about that?"

"My focus isn't your wedding. I have nothing to do with the sabotage."

Even Mr. Keep-to-the-Shadows thought it was sabotage.

Maybe he knew the identity of the waste of space stalking her wedding? "Got any information about the sabotage? I'd like to get married without any other dead bodies popping up."

Liam backed away, hands held up. "Like I said, I have nothing to do with the wedding. I told you that."

"No. But you might have some ideas. And you're following someone who also has a connection to my wedding and maybe the sabotage. My great-uncle Edgar."

"I'm just here on holiday. That's all."

"Uh-huh." Xandie nodded and tapped her chin thoughtfully. "We aren't idiots. And we have experience with agents going off the book. Trust me. You have that thousand-yard stare down pat."

A small puddle of golden light from the police station illuminated Liam's face in the dark night. He grimaced and rubbed his buzz cut head with a surprisingly elegant motion of his hand.

Xandie pressed. "Look, if you're in trouble, we can help. That's what we do. The Harrows, I mean."

He let out a sharp bark of laughter. "What I've observed is that you're all about causing chaos."

"That too. But we have a knack for solving problems, as well as the odd mystery or two. Why not make it easier and just tell us?"

"That's not how I work." Liam inclined his head and marched down the cobblestone streets away from the police station, disappearing into the dark.

"We'll find out what's going on, and we'll help you whether or not you want it. Just keep that in mind," Xandie bellowed.

"Is there a reason you're yelling in the street, in the middle of the night, Alexandra?"

Nicolas stood framed in the police station entrance, his elegant navy-blue suit unruffled despite the late hour.

Xandie pasted on a weak smile and faced her father. "Would you believe I was offering to help someone?"

"With all the time you spend with Elspeth, nothing surprises me." He speared his daughter with a stern look. "I'm aware you're busy stalking murderers and breaking into stores, but I'd like to remind you about our morning tea at Mayweather Inn tomorrow. I will accept no excuses for tardiness. Mandatory attendance."

"Morning tea. *Yay.*" Rose Mayweather and an enforced morning tea with her father, mother, and future mother-in-law. Just what she needed after a night at the police station.

"You get sandwiches and water." Rose Mayweather dumped a plate of finger sandwiches in the middle of the table. "You have a range of smoked trout, cucumber, lobster, and egg. Blueberry muffins and almond teacakes are coming. We're having problems with power fluctuations and wiring issues. So, morning tea is a basic set menu." Rose glared. "The sooner we get you married off, the better for everybody." The inn owner stomped out of the dining room, salmon pink petticoats frothing around her legs.

Xandie said nothing, just raised her eyebrows and cast a quick look at her mother and Aggie, Zach's mom. Unfortunately, Xandie agree with Rose. The sooner this marriage took place, the better for everyone.

"That woman wouldn't know the meaning of customer service if it knocked her overdone blonde wig off her head." Xandie's father sniffed, selected a finger sandwich, and slid it onto his plate. "At least the bed is comfortable, and the food looks relatively fresh, I suppose."

"Considering how Rose feels about Harrows, we're lucky she's serving us at all. Not to mention hosting my wedding in her garden." Xandie grabbed a sandwich and took a large bite, humming as eggy goodness hit her tongue. Not as good as chocolate, but not bad.

"I am not surprised you have an appetite, considering your escapades last night."

It wasn't too hard to tell that her father disapproved of her activities from the tone of his voice. "Zach knew where we were and what we were doing. It's not our fault someone showed up with nefarious motives."

Aggie took the opportunity to jump in. "Everyone a Harrow has ever upset probably has nefarious motives. But that kid's definitely a mystery."

"What do you mean?" He was a stalker all right, but Xandie had a feeling the mystery revolved around the Harrows.

"The boy asked for a phone call as soon as he sat his tush on the interview chair. Lickety-split, Zachy bear receives a call from on high, telling us to release him."

"Who are the people on high?" On high could mean anything from military, government, and law enforcement to gods and goddesses. Xandie needed specifics. She had a Harrow bad feeling it was important.

"Defense directorate and the paranormal investigator group." Aggie took a bite, chewing slowly. "You know, something about that man feels familiar."

Thank Hecate she wasn't the only one. "Yes." Xandie slapped the table and pointed at Aggie. "Future mother-in-law points to you. I'm thinking the same thing."

"Maybe he has one of those faces? And I'll bank those

mother-in-law points. You never know when I might need them." Aggie winked.

"A familiar face isn't an asset in his type of job."

"Black ops?"

Miranda cocked her head. "I bet sniper of some sort. My contact had a peek at his file. Most of it's blacked out. But I've got a last name. Munro. Liam Munro, but I'd lay down money that's an alias."

"We're talking about the young man who was picked up along with the rest of you delinquents?"

"That's the guy. We've been seeing him around town wherever Elspeth's brother is."

Xandie's father grimaced. His face looked like he'd sucked on a lemon. It was his *I-have-information-but-I-don't-want-to-encourage-you* expression. "Spit it out, Dad. I know you know something."

"I hate encouraging your Sherlockian behavior, but needs must, I suppose." He inclined his salt-and-pepper-colored head at his daughter. "I have seen the young man around the inn. Seems innocuous but he's very interested not just in Edgar Harrow but his partner as well. Especially when they bickered over their finances."

"What about finances?" Gigi struck Xandie as a high-maintenance fashion lover.

"Edgar doesn't approve of his fiancée's spending habits. Apparently, she has expensive tastes. I also think that young man may have searched their rooms."

"What makes you think that, Dad?"

"I saw him in the second-floor hallway as I passed him. When I turned to watch what he was doing a few seconds later, he'd disappeared, and he hadn't passed me. The room he lurked outside of belongs to Edgar Harrow. He and his fiancée do not share accommodation." Nicolas sat back, a satisfied smile upon his face. "Now that's out of the way, I want to discuss the issue of your wedding and bridesmaids' dresses."

She needed to get to Edgar and Gigi's rooms and search them. Xandie hated playing catch up, and Liam was one step ahead of her. "Elspeth's lending me her dress."

Aggie let out a bark of laughter. "She won it at a poker game, from a witch who'd been stabbed by her groom on their wedding day. The witch swore the dress was cursed. Elspeth loved it."

"No. Absolutely not." Nicolas glowered at the table. "I will not permit my only child to be married in a cursed, secondhand dress. I have another option for both you and the bridesmaids."

Xandie held up her hand. "Could we table the dress discussion for later? I need to get to Edgar and Gigi's rooms and go over them."

"Great idea, sweet girl." Aggie grinned from ear to ear. "Your mother and I can stand look out." She rubbed her hands. "This reminds me of the escapades your grandmother and I went on when we were younger."

"The less we know about that, the better." Miranda stood. "Let's get this done before Mayweather clues into what we're doing." Xandie's mother reached into a pocket and drew out a gray-colored key. "This might come in handy."

"Great-Aunt Rose's finger key? How did you snatch that from Elspeth? Aunt Winifred made me give it back." Xandie took the key with a grimace. Using her great-aunt's finger bone that had been carved into a skeleton key by Elspeth at some stage gave her the ick factor.

Miranda just smiled. "I made my own copy years ago."

"Man, I have the smartest mother in the world." Xandie

held the skeleton up and released a deep breath. "I need someone on the stairs watching for Rose and someone to deliver the warning to me while I'm searching the room."

"I bag the stairs. I can pretend I'm taking a call." Aggie stood. "Let's do this." She stomped out of the dining room.

Nicolas sniffed. "I gather my presence isn't required? If that's the case, I'll remain at the table." He pinned Xandie with a stern gaze. "We *will* revisit the dress issue at another time. Understand me, Alexandra?"

"Later, Dad." Xandie waved her father off and casually sauntered out, passing Aggie on the stairs, who pretended to take a call.

Miranda kept pace with her daughter, then stopped halfway down the hall and leaned against a door. "This is your father's room. I'll stay here like I'm waiting for him. It's close enough I can warn you. Don't take too long. Edgar and Gigi's rooms are two doors down, next to each other. Their assistant is across from them."

Xandie nodded her understanding. She knocked on Edgar's door and waited for an answer that wasn't forthcoming. Using the copy of her great aunt Rose's finger, she let herself into his room. His very clean and organized room. She shuddered. Elspeth always said clean room, crazy mind. Maybe her grandmother wasn't far off. Xandie poked through the wardrobe. Three suits, all sporting threadbare, worn patches, hung in the mostly empty wardrobe. She checked all the pockets, but they were empty even of lint. An open suitcase sat at the base of the wardrobe, and she rifled through it but came up with zero.

"Edgar equals nothing," Xandie muttered, but took another tour of the room, this time stopping at a partially filled wastepaper basket. She searched through and pulled up a scrunched ball of paper. Unfolding it, she scanned it.

"Edgar's running on empty." The bank statement highlighted Gigi's over the top spending. Rose Mayweather might as well put her great-uncle to work washing up in the kitchen because there was no way he'd be able to pay for their accommodation. Xandie hid the statement away and moved to the hallway, poking her head out to see if the coast was clear.

Miranda nodded casually, and Xandie repeated the process of knocking on Gigi's door, then letting herself in.

Gigi's room was the exact opposite of her fiancé's. Chaos in the form of fashion reigned supreme. Dresses, skirts, tops, and underwear lay draped over every available surface. A sea of shoes covered one side of the room, and lotions and beauty products exploded across the desk. Xandie checked the wastebasket, but Gigi's was empty. "I can see why old Edgar's broke." Giving up on Gigi's room, Xandie moved to the assistant's.

Malcolm was a combination of Edgar and Gigi. Xandie peered into the wardrobe full of expensive looking suits. "Assistants must be paid well if you can afford all those brands." Like Gigi, an explosion of men's shoes covered the floor on one side of the bed. Xandie used a sneaker-clad foot to move the shoes around. "These shoes are a big size, but Malcolm looks so slim and small." She never expected such a large shoe from just looking at him.

A sharp knock on the door froze Xandie until she heard her mother's voice. "Xandie, you need to finish up. We have a problem."

It's Point Muse. Of course there's a problem. Giving up on Malcolm's rooms, Xandie stepped out into the hallway. Miranda had left her post and stood with Aggie at the top of the stairs.

High-pitched screeching floated upward.

Wincing, Xandie joined her mother and soon-to-be mother-in-law. "Let me guess. Another Harrow-caused catastrophe has beset Mayweather Inn?"

"Judging by the cursing we've heard, something has happened to the rose garden."

"The rose garden? The garden where my wedding's supposed to happen? *That garden?*" Xandie's own voice joined Rose Mayweather's shrieking tones.

Miranda raised her hand. "I'm sure your wedding will be fine. It's just another hiccup we'll deal with."

That's it. Xandie was done. Tapped out. Eloping was officially taking top billing. That or cancel the whole shebang and live in sin in her library.

Wouldn't Elspeth love that...

FOURTEEN

"Duck. "

Holly prostrated herself flat on the floor, hands crossed over the back of her head. "Am I good? Is it all clear?"

"*Eh.*" Xandie shrugged and drummed her fingers on her desk, watching cream-colored parchment scrolls dual over her cousin's head. The Library lights overhead flickered off and on like rabid disco lights, trying to distract her from her wedding catastrophe. *It isn't working.* "I'm calling the whole shebang off. My wedding is kaput. The Library won't care if we live in sin here."

Holly rolled over and stared at Xandie. "Seriously?"

Xandie nodded. "I'm done. Dipped in chocolate and freeze dried. Completely done. We can stay engaged for the rest of our lives." She crossed her arms and dared her family to comment.

Taking up the challenge first, Zach winked at his fiancée. "Anything you want. As long as no more dead bodies are involved, the Library and I are here for you."

"I'm not." Theo strolled in through the door that connected the rest of the house to the Library. "I want my time on your wedding karaoke stage. I need to shine like the star I am."

"You get hairballs and cough them into unsuspecting shoes. You don't get a vote." Xandie pouted and sprawled over her desk, head now resting on top of her crossed arms. "I don't care what anyone else says."

Aggie narrowed her eyes. "No one?"

Annoyed bear shifter alert. Xandie straightened and smiled sweetly. "Except my maybe-not-so-soon-to-be mother-in-law."

"I'll support you, whatever you decide, as long as..." Aggie smirked. "You give me a lifetime supply of honey buns."

"Done." *So easily bought.* "My supplier will be in contact with you."

"Will I?" Lila lounged on the couch, kicking her foot up and down.

"No, you will not." Elspeth stormed past Lila and flicked her on the back of the head. "Don't enable her. This is just a knee-jerk reaction to stress. You should be encouraging her to stand up and face her anxiety." Elspeth glared at Xandie, her bright pink mullet on show as she shook her head. "No granddaughter of mine's going down in flames whimpering. We fight until we burn out."

"How violent." Holly stood and dusted her jeans. "But since it's Xandie's jinxed wedding, shouldn't it be her final decision?"

"No one derails my wedding plans," Elspeth barked. "My reputation as Point Muse's pre-eminent event planner is on the line. Edgar will not best me."

Felicity cleared her throat. "I hate to burst the wedding bubble, but we don't have a backup plan since the

Mayweather Inn is refusing to have us anywhere near their grounds now."

"And I refuse to leave this Library." Xandie stuck out her bottom lip. If a bride couldn't get away with a pout or two, there was no justice in the world.

Cackling, Elspeth clapped her hands. "And that's why I'm paid the big bucks. I have a backup. The best backup ever designed for an exclusive, one-of-a-kind wedding event."

"When was she paid the big bucks?"

"In her very own small mind. Probably in virtual cash," Lila whispered back to Holly.

Ignoring their mocking barbs, Elspeth pointed outside. "If the Librarian won't leave the Library for the wedding, how about the wedding comes to the Librarian?"

"From a security standpoint, that's an effective strategy," Miranda admitted from her post against a far wall. "The Library can protect the wedding party and its guests inside or outside. I can work in conjunction with it and tailor a security package."

"I guess it could work." Xandie looked over at Zach, who winked at her again.

"Like I said. Anything you want..."

"As long as it includes honey buns." Aggie beamed. "You have to admit, the witch rolls with the punches and comes up with genius."

Sticking her nose in the air, Elspeth preened. "I *am* awesome."

Books rattled on shelves, and scrolls flew around the room, narrowly avoiding heads. Xandie peeked out the windows and spotted multiple rosebushes in sudden bloom. Cobblestones appeared around the statues of the nine muses that stood in the middle of the garden. "You already mentioned this to the Library, didn't you? That's why it's been frisky all morning."

"I may have mentioned it in passing when I arrived."

Elspeth and her pre-emptive anxiety strike. "Fine. The Library can host the wedding."

"We still have the problem of music and bridesmaids' dresses." Felicity checked the wedding book. "Food can be handled by the family, as is the wedding dress." The wedding assistant grimaced but continued, "Flowers are being dealt with by Winifred Harrow, but what about the vows? *And* we have no music."

"Au contraire, my little wedding minion." Elspeth drew herself up. "I have completed a celebrant's course, and I am completely qualified to marry Harrow and Braun."

"Meyers." Xandie's half-hearted utterance was waved away.

"I've also employed a magical cellist. His wedding march is to die for, and he's experienced with magical attacks, so you can add him to the security package."

"What?" Miranda pushed herself away from the wall. "Are you talking about Windsor Shaw?"

"The only possible choice for an elegant wedding."

"Nope. No way." Miranda stalked toward her mother. "Not at my daughter's wedding."

Xandie braced herself. "Okay. Give it to me. What's wrong with him?"

"He's a magical assassin. Currently wanted in half a dozen countries for murder."

"He's misunderstood. Shaw's a nice boy who owes me a favor. Plus, he'll wear a nullifying band. No killing with music."

Miranda threw up her hands and headed back to her

wall. She thumped her head against it a few times for good measure.

"I'm not thrilled about a wanted musical assassin at our wedding. But if the band works and Elspeth goes guarantor on his murderous behavior, then I'm good to go. If you are, Xandie?"

Elspeth was a pretty good deterrent all by herself. "Fine, but it's on your head if something happens." Xandie pointed to her grandmother. "I don't want to hear about any murderous-assassin-cellist-related issues. Got me?"

Elspeth flipped a cross over her chest. "Cross my heart. Everything will be stress-free after this."

The Library door slammed open, rebounding against the wall. Two older women with bright-colored, curly wigs stood framed in the doorway. One of the women held up what looked to be a severed head. "We have a problem."

The other woman, wearing a wig of fluorescent green curls, shrieked, "It's the wig Apocalypse."

"Not even five seconds. That's a record. Even for Elspeth." Theo strutted over to the women. "Did a kid's crayon box explode on your head, or are you color blind? Your brightness offends me." The cat stalked past the women, his tail slapping them left and right as he left.

"Come on in, Dorothy and Olive. Lay the next calamity upon me. I'm sure someone here can take me out if I have a mental break." Xandie waved the town's hairdressers, and Elspeth's cronies, in.

Wearing a bright yellow wig, Dorothy stepped in and hoisted a hairy, melted object into the air. "It's kaput. Flat-lined. There's no hope of saving it. I'm so sorry, Elspeth."

Elspeth hissed and slapped a trembling hand over her mouth.

Olive, Dorothy's sister-in-law, sobbed dramatically. "We

opened early today so we could style your wig for the wedding and found the shop trashed, every wig burned and ripped apart. And then we found that sacrilege." She shook the melted monstrosity she held high. "Still melting like the wicked witch from Oz."

Dorothy carefully passed the wig to Elspeth, who cradled it. "We respect your loss." She bowed her head for a moment. "We'll try get some more wigs in, hopefully in time for Xandie's wedding."

Tears gathered in the corners of Elspeth's eyes as she pulled the destroyed wig to her bony chest. "This is a strike against a woman's essence. My very femininity. This is a desecration that will have a swift and vicious retaliation." Elspeth's voice trembled. "It's on like Donkey Kong."

"Here." Olive handed Xandie a plain white business card. "This guy with way too much product in his hair came in yesterday. Wanted to buy all our wigs. We told him to bug off, but he left the card in case we changed our mind. It could be a clue."

Dorothy snorted. "As if we'd ever listen to someone that over-produced. It affects the brain, you know. Makes you pick poor life choices."

Aggie stood and shared a look with her son before hustling over to the hairdressers. "Why don't we head to your store and take inventory? Zachy bear will follow us and take a report. We'll track the wig-hater down and throw the book at him."

Braun stepped up next to Xandie and lowered his voice. "Don't let this stress you. It's a wig. I'm sure Elspeth can find another for the wedding."

"It's not the destroyed wig. Well..." Xandie amended her words. "For Elspeth, it is. But for me, it's the malice behind it. Someone really wanted to take a jab at her." She fingered the business card that Olive had given her. Xandie knew exactly what was on it. James Neville, lawyer.

"Whatever you do, take someone other than Elspeth with you. Someone partially sane works for me." Zach leaned forward and brushed a gentle kiss over Xandie's nose. "Keep in touch and be safe." He followed his mother and the overwrought hairdressers out of the room.

"Goodness." Felicity blew out a breath. "Is it always like this in the Harrow family?"

"You mean drama, tears, and melted wigs?" Lila sat up and shrugged. "Harrows equal mayhem. There's always a chance of drama with tears."

A high-pitched warbling filled the air. The room's occupants winced in unison.

"Sorry. That would be Theo, practicing his voice exercises." Xandie winced at an excruciatingly high-pitched note.

Felicity slammed the wedding book shut. "On that really high note, I need to head home as I have some personal issues that need attending to. I'll leave you to cope with non-wedding related karaoke tunes. I'm sure everything will be fine now that you've picked the Library as the wedding venue." Felicity nodded encouragingly at Xandie before she left.

Xandie showed the card to Lila. "I think I see a Portland trip in our immediate future. Like in the next few minutes."

"Getting out of Point Muse probably isn't a bad idea." Miranda picked up a notepad from a shelf. "I'll stay here. Go through the Library and house and note down security issues. We've got this." Miranda disappeared through the open door.

"Okay, everyone has a gameplan then."

Holly held up her hand. "I don't. What do I do?"

Elspeth slapped a hand over her granddaughter's mouth. "You're with me, banshee. We have a mission." She dragged Holly toward the door.

Elspeth's hand slipped away as Holly tried to wiggle free. "Don't let her take me to a secondary location," Holly yelled over Elspeth's admonitions to stay calm.

"Stop fighting the inevitable, Holly. You are now Elspeth's minion. Wallow in your handiness," Lila bellowed, then broke into hysterical giggling.

Some days, Harrows and sanity only had a passing acquaintance.

FIFTEEN

"No scratches and we weren't forced off the road and threatened. This is a first." Lila clapped Xandie on the back. "Maybe your wedding luck is changing."

"The day hasn't finished yet." Xandie checked the address on the back of the card.

"Aren't you a gloomy Librarian? You have to stay positive."

"I'm positive the way my wedding is looking, we'll find another body soon. How's that?"

"Not quite what I had in mind."

"It should be around here somewhere." They were near the harbor and the older part of Portland. Old Port was an historic area with cobblestone streets and boutique clothing stores that jostled with souvenir shops, pubs, cafés, and cocktail bars, all housed in quaint brick buildings.

"You looking for someone in particular, girls?"

An older woman with frizzy gray hair piled on top of her head in a messy bun sat at a small wrought iron table in front of a trendy looking café.

"Looking for the office of James Neville, lawyer."

"Ha," the older woman snorted. "You mean James Neville Rowbotham. Although, come to think of it, he did drop the Rowbotham a little while ago. Not marketable enough apparently."

"Why does a lawyer need to be marketable?" Xandie shoved the card back in her jeans pocket.

"A lawyer doesn't, but an actor does." The woman patted the chair next to her. "Sit on down if you want to talk."

Taking the invitation, Xandie dropped into the chair and Lila followed suit. "I'm Xandie. And this is my cousin, Lila."

"Hannah, at your service." She winked. "Why are you looking for James? You cops?"

"Our grandmother would drown us if we strayed to the dark side." Lila smirked. "But it might be worth the entertainment value."

"My granddaughters live to annoy me too." Hannah waved behind her at the café. "I own the building, and they run the café. James rented space above the café from me."

"And he's an actor, not a lawyer?" That kind of made sense. Reading from a notebook like he was memorizing lines. Always looking to Gigi and Edgar for reassurance. It was all a part.

"He's got his office set up like a lawyer, with certificates on the wall. But if you look closer, you can see they're just printed out. He even has a watermark from a stock photo website on one of them." Hannah shook her head. "Boy just can't get things right."

"How long has he been leasing space for?"

"The last six months or so. I thought he was setting it up for some kind of method acting. You know, play a lawyer so you immerse yourself in a lawyer's life?"

Lila leaned her elbows on the table. "Why so sure he's an actor?"

"Because he showed me some head shots a while ago. Asked me which one I preferred. Then he clammed up, like he realized he had made a mistake or stepped out of character. I've heard him running lines as well. And he's only ever had one client that I saw."

"Let me guess. An older man with amber eyes?"

Edgar Harrow. Elspeth would have a field day when she found out his lawyer was a fake.

"Nope. A fake redhead with ridiculous shoes. She had to take the heels off to get upstairs. Why women subject themselves to that I have no clue. Sensible is the way to go." She shoved a dark blue orthopedic shoe out from underneath the table. "Not so pretty, but it's like walking on a cloud."

"Would you mind if we had a look at the office upstairs?"

"Knock yourselves out." Hannah heaved herself up. "Come on." She opened a slim door next to the café, exposing a narrow set of stairs.

Reaching the top corner, Hannah led them down a dimly lit hallway until they reached a door with the name of James Neville stenciled on the frosted glass.

"Don't expect much." Hannah unlocked the door and opened it. "James isn't a decorating guy, unless it comes to himself and excess product."

Hannah wasn't wrong. The office only held a battered wooden desk, half a dozen very fake certificates framed on the wall, a lumpy couch, and a small gray metal filing cabinet under the desk. Dust covered every available surface. James Neville, fake lawyer, hadn't been here in a while.

Lila tapped a certificate. "You're right about the watermark. He doesn't even bother to remove it. He's just added his name to the certificate and printed it out."

"No kidding." Xandie opened the small, two-drawer filing cabinet and pulled out a glossy headshot of their fake lawyer with the name James Neville scored across the bottom in black marker. "You'd think he'd hide these photos if he's pretending to be a lawyer."

"Told you. He isn't the brightest spark. But he's paid up for another two weeks. Then I'll clear this place, clean it, and rent it back out again."

"Did he mention anything about Point Muse or the Harrows?"

"Not to me, but he spoke to my girls a bit. He loves his coffee." Hannah rattled the keys. "You seen enough?"

Lila smiled at the older woman. "We'll talk to your granddaughters downstairs. Thanks for your help." She followed Xandie down the stairs.

"You see James, let him know he's got two weeks to clear his stuff out and then I'll sell it."

"Will do." Xandie waved to the woman as the girls trudged back downstairs and into the small café.

A plump, red-cheeked woman in her late twenties, long blonde hair tied up in a high, perky ponytail, smiled at them. "What can I get you?"

"Your grandmother sent us to speak to you. We're trying to find information about James Neville Rowbotham. Or whatever his name is currently." Xandie drew out the business card and showed it to the woman behind the counter.

The woman rolled her eyes. "I warned him that was a bad idea, but he wouldn't listen to me. It was all part of the job."

"Acting or lawyering?" Lila leaned against the counter.

"Your pastries look great, by the way. I own a bakery in Point Muse, so I know my baked goods."

Beaming, the woman slid two small pastries on a plate. She handed them to Lila. "Goat cheese and leek croissants. My sister has a light touch with pastry."

"Yummo." Lila waved Xandie on. "I'll just stand here and taste-test. Ask your questions, Sherlock Librarian."

"Family." Xandie shook her head. "So, is James an actor or a lawyer?"

"Definitely an actor, but he's not a great one. He chats to us whenever he grabs a coffee. He's been out of work for so long, he's willing to do anything."

"Like impersonating a lawyer?"

"Like that." She nodded. "I think he lucked into some big payday. He just had to pretend he was a lawyer for a while. Maybe a road trip or two. Someplace on the coast."

"Point Muse maybe?"

She snapped her fingers. "That's the place. He expects a big payday. And then he'll pay us back for all the free coffee he's drunk. I thought it was an acting job and asked if we'd see him on television. But he just laughed, said he hoped, but it would pay well." She shrugged. "That's all I've got. He isn't a real lawyer, and I'm pretty sure he's fallen into some sort of dodgy scheme for cash. But that's James for you. Always looking for the next payday."

What it boiled down to was that James Neville Rowbotham was a fake. Elspeth would be rubbing her hands and cackling when she found out. "Thanks for your help."

"No worries. I hope you sort out your problem. James is an idiot, but he's nice enough."

Lila grabbed the last goat cheese croissant and waved

goodbye. Xandie towed her cousin outside. "These really are good. We could have them at your wedding reception."

"I'd rather focus on getting back to Point Muse in one piece."

"And letting Elspeth know that James Neville, Esquire, isn't a real lawyer."

"That too."

Xandie concealed a yawn behind her hand. Night had fallen, and the old-fashioned streetlamps lining the Main Street of Point Muse illuminated very little.

"Zach's meeting you?"

"Probably pacing the alley behind the bakery as we speak. He hates the idea of me being out and about at night with a killer stalking our wedding."

"And of course, he's worried about your favorite cousin too. Right?"

"Yep, let's go with that."

Lila pulled into the alley and slowly came to a stop. The bakery van's headlights illuminated a figure crouched over a dark mass sprawled on the ground.

"He isn't pacing at least."

Xandie opened the van door and slipped out as the crouching figure stood and turned to face them.

"Isn't this when you normally say to me...*what a surprise to see you at my crime scene?*"

"It's my crime scene now." Zach stepped forward into the reflected light from the headlights. "I guess it had to be my turn sometime to find a dead body."

Lila peeked around her open van door. "Let me guess. That's the fake lawyer in my alley, isn't it?"

"I don't know about the fake bit, but he's dead. He had a bottle of vitamins shoved in his mouth. I'm betting choked to death, but I'll know more after my crime scene brownies have been through. I've already called it in. They're on the way."

"Bottle of vitamins in his throat and Edgar Harrow sells vitamins. Plus, the dead guy wasn't a lawyer but an actor. Seems to be pointing to one person."

Her cousin was right. And wouldn't Elspeth launch into her victory twerk when she found out. There was no controlling a victorious Elspeth.

SIXTEEN

"Is there such a thing as a wedding jinx? Because I really feel my wedding has an ominous going-down-with-the-ship Titanic vibe to it." Xandie paced in the center of the sitting room at Harrow House. "I mean, look at all the wedding-connected bodies. The sabotage. And I can't even get a feel for the situation and suspects like I normally would," Xandie growled and tugged at her frizzy, brown hair. If she didn't stop the killer soon, no one would be attending the wedding. *Maybe that's a good idea.* Xandie hadn't realized she'd spoken aloud until Elspeth leaped over and grabbed her by the shoulder, shaking her as she spoke.

"Snap out of the woe-is-me black hole. Go toward the light." Elspeth stopped and frowned. "That isn't right, is it?"

Lila spat her coffee out, spraying Holly, who also squealed and put her hands over her head like it was raining.

"Say it, don't spray it. Think of all the germs that just spread through the air."

"Deal with it, germaphobe." Lila carefully placed her coffee on a small side table. "Please, Xandie. Don't go toward the light. In this equation, the light is *not* a good thing."

"Stop your sassing, baker girl, or you're on my list." Elspeth pointed a finger at Lila before swiveling and jabbing it at Xandie. "No cancelling. In fact, you're having two weddings. So, suck it up, buttercup. Deal with it. Your first wedding is tomorrow night. Here at Harrow House."

"It's hard enough organizing one, let alone two. Are you sipping witch shine, old woman?" Xandie slapped hands on her hips and glared at her grandmother. "Do you know the amount of stress I'm under right now?"

"Settle down, bridezilla. The first wedding is a trap." Elspeth rubbed her hands together. "Edgar won't be able to resist, then bam." She slapped her hands together. "I've got him, and you can have your second stress-free wedding, planned by the pre-eminent Point Muse wedding planner. It's perfect." Xandie's grandmother faced the rest of the room. "Heap your praise upon me. I can take it."

"Are you high on your own herbs?" Holly stared at Elspeth. "This will end badly, probably with me catching a horribly disfiguring plague caused by your love of chaos and mayhem."

"It isn't a horrible idea as long as it's planned right." Miranda arched an eyebrow. "I'm assuming you've spent time on your plan specifics?"

Elspeth curled her lip. "What do you think I am, an amateur?"

"Nope. I'm out." Xandie scuttled forward and made the sitting-room doorway before her mother snagged her.

"Let's just listen to her plan first. Okay, sweetie?"

"Fine," Xandie grumbled but stayed put. She spotted Felicity pacing up and down the hallway, whispering on her phone. The assistant's secret affair must be heating up. At least something was going right for someone else.

"Are you listening? You whined about a plan. So, here it is."

"I'm listening, geez." Xandie gritted her teeth. Someone else needed to get married and experience her pain.

"Felicity and I have planned it all out. We'll set up the garden here with a fake wedding scene. Seats laid out, a trellis with flowers. I even have our own flower supplier supplying us with rose petals for along the aisle. Braun can be dressed in some cheap suit and wait at the altar with his handcuffs. You don't even have to show. In fact, it'll be better if you don't." Elspeth licked her lips, anticipating victory. "Edgar won't be able to help himself. He'll try to sabotage the wedding, and then I'll close the trap. I've already sent invites out to some of our friends to make it look real."

"That's why you haven't been lurking around like normal. You've been plotting," Xandie accused.

Felicity stepped up next to Xandie. "Elspeth and I made a point to consider all areas of safety. We both agree this is the only way you'll have a stress-free wedding." Felicity held out a notepad. "I took notes if anyone is interested."

Miranda grabbed the notebook. "I'll take that."

Xandie groaned. Tomorrow night would end badly. She felt it in her Harrow bones.

"I thought the florist was supplying flower petals for the aisle?" Xandie peeked out through a small gap in the curtain. "Those petals look fake and tacky. I mean, who chooses purple and green as a color scheme for a wedding?"

"You're mocking your own fake wedding? That's weird, even for a Harrow." Lila joined Xandie in peeking out the window. "But Braun looks good, even in a lilac suit. What costume shop did he raid to find that?"

"Evidence locker. It's from a closed case."

Her fiancé even made pastel look handsome. She stifled a giggle. Laughing at your own fake wedding probably wasn't correct wedding etiquette. "I'm just saying, even though it's a fake wedding, I still have standards."

"Here's hoping you get to show off your standards at your real wedding." Lila pressed closer, peering through the gap in the curtain. "Guests have arrived. Mostly Point Muse residents and Elspeth's cronies. I think half of them are packing hip flasks judging by the suspiciously shaped bulges in their pockets."

"It's Point Muse. I'm not staring at any suspicious bulges. I'd probably end up hexed." Xandie switched to another window, facing the porch. "Has anyone seen Elspeth?"

"She's lurking in her creation cave, ready to leap out when Edgar turns up, I guess. Aunt Winifred's sitting in the crowd, and your dad refused to participate, and my mom wants Elspeth to stew in her own mayhem. So, she's turning up late so she can see the action unfold."

"And my mom's on the porch, standing watch." Miranda's back faced Xandie close enough she watched her mother's muscles clench as she shifted on the spot.

"Any sign of Aggie yet?" Lila joined Xandie at the window.

"Nope, but I think Holly's forcing someone to go to my fake wedding with her."

Lila shrugged, unconcerned. "You do what you gotta do when you're a single banshee."

Holly shoved a man onto the porch and grabbed Miranda's arm, speaking urgently to her before they both grabbed the man.

"What's going on? A security risk? Is he part of Elspeth's trap?"

Xandie shrugged. "I have no clue what's going on."

The man raised his face. Xandie recognized Liam, her alley rescuer and fellow police station visitor. "That's Liam. He must be following Edgar and thinks he'll turn up here for the wedding."

Without warning, Harrow House's front door swung open with a resounding bang, and the porch floor rippled. Miranda and Holly wavered on their feet, and Liam steadied them. The house shook again, and the trio on the porch stumbled into the hallway. The front door slammed shut behind them.

"What the heckadoodles are you all doing in here? I have a trap to spring, and I can't hear through the clamoring of the house." Elspeth stood at the head of the hallway, resplendent in a shiny white jogging suit with matching combat boots and a pale lilac, chin-length bob with a feathery, blunt fringe.

"Don't look at us. The house went crazy when Holly dragged her fake wedding date onto the porch." Xandie pointed at Liam. "Somehow, she got the Edgar stalker to fake date her."

"Hey," Holly protested. "It's not a fake date or any kind of date. I found him lurking and brought him in."

"She grabbed me and threatened to get Elspeth to hex my underwear drawer shut if I didn't follow her. And I'm not a wedding crasher. I was invited."

Xandie frowned. "By whom?"

"That would be me. The enemy of my enemy is my ally." Elspeth smirked. "You lot need to smarten up. You're severely disappointing me."

Liam raised his face and peered around the entranceway of Harrow House before fixing his gaze back on Elspeth. "I'm not an enemy of Edgar's or yours." The skin of his face rippled for a moment, and the blue of his eyes leached out until nothing but amber glowed.

As one, the Harrows inhaled and stared.

"Mystical male Harrows are coming out of the woodwork," Lila gaped, then closed her mouth. "Harrow House must have realized as soon as he stood on the porch and broke his glamor."

Elspeth clomped up to Liam and shook her finger in his face. "See this finger? It's loaded and ready to fire, as is my pug, who's probably lurking in the kitchen with the fake reception food."

Liam took a step back, hands held up. "I'm not here to cause issues. I'm just trying to protect my grandfather."

"Edgar." Elspeth hissed her brother's name.

"You know what? I don't have a death wish. I'm heading outside to keep watch." Holly slapped Liam on the back as she scooted past. "Welcome to the crazy Harrow clan, fresh meat..." Holly amended her words. "I mean cousin." She slipped out the door without a backward glance.

"Rats always desert a sinking ship first," Lila muttered.

"You're Edgar's grandson. Why do you need to protect him, and why didn't you tell us you were a Harrow?"

Liam rubbed the side of his shaved head at Xandie's question. "My father won't have anything to do with Edgar. And I've been away since I signed up with the army. I'm out now and freelancing."

"Sniper?"

"When I'm needed." Liam nodded at Miranda. "I have a habit of hitting every target I aim for. Handy in some areas."

Miranda nodded back, a small smile twitching the corners of her mouth. "Kinetic sight. It runs in the family."

"What about that nefarious Edgar? Why does he need protection?" Elspeth glowered at the young man.

"Dad doesn't get on with Edgar, but he's an accountant and keeps an eye on the old man's finances. Grandad's fiancée is bleeding him dry. I'm here to suss out the situation."

"Ha," Elspeth crowed. "I knew the old blowhard was after money."

"The vitamin business did well, until Gigi turned up. I tracked them here and have been keeping an eye out."

"Seen anything interesting?" Cousin Liam might turn out useful.

"Just that Gigi's a gold-digger and could talk Edgar into anything. He isn't the killer. He's great with threats but poor on follow-up."

"Except he's up to his neck in something. That lawyer he employed? He was an out of work actor."

"*Was?*"

Xandie nodded at her new cousin. "We checked him out in Portland and when we arrived back in town, found him dead in an alleyway with a bottle of vitamins shoved in his mouth."

"Nope. No. Wasn't my grandfather." Liam shook his head.

Holly poked her head back into the house. "We have an Edgar sighting. I repeat. We have Edgar incoming."

"She needs to stop watching spy and war movies. It gives her too many ideas."

"What evs. But Edgar and Gigi just rocked up. And stop insulting me."

"Let me at that mongoose." Elspeth shoved past the family and out onto the porch, hollering Edgar's name. Raised voices drifted into the sitting room.

"That's my cue to disappear. I don't want Grandad spotting me just yet." Liam blended back into the shadowed hallway. Harrow House increased the darkness around him until he matched his surroundings.

"Harrow House likes him. It's kind of nice to have fresh blood in the family for Elspeth to torture."

Xandie agreed with Lila. It was nice to have Elspeth focus on someone else.

"The situation has escalated. *I repeat.* The situation threat level has escalated," Holly screeched from outside.

Something pink flew past the partially open door, and a massive thunk sounded from outside, followed by Harrow House shifting.

"I'll report you for assault. Do you hear me?" Gigi's strident voice cut through Elspeth's cackles.

"You know what? This is my fake wedding, and I think Liam has the right idea. I'm staying out of it." Xandie bared her teeth in a predator's false smile and shoved her cousin out the door, slamming it shut behind her. Xandie yelled through the door, "Good luck, Lila. I'm sure you and Holly can handle a cackling Elspeth and a pink-gooped Edgar and Gigi. It can be your fake wedding present to me."

"Right now, I'm concerned you inherited more of Elspeth's genes then you should have."

Xandie winked at her mother. "A bride should always enjoy her fake wedding day."

SEVENTEEN

"Two days of peace and no assault charge. Surely, I should be happy? So, why am I filled with a sense of impending doom?" Xandie grabbed a glass and chugged the contents back, wiping her mouth on her sleeve.

"Whoa. Hitting the hard stuff early. You should slow down, or you won't last the night." Lila grabbed Xandie's glass and filled it back up with chocolate milk. "But I suppose if you can't let go of your non-alcoholic sweet tooth at your combined bachelor and bachelorette party, when can you?"

Xandie glanced around the large front room at the Brauns' Lodge. *Think log cabin on steroids.* Generations ago, the Brauns had emigrated from the Black Forest in Germany and settled on a tree-filled acreage in Point Muse. Perfect for the bear shifters. "At least everyone's having fun." Her mom and dad were huddled in a corner cuddling. The Braun brothers were competing against their sister and mother with a board game...*loudly*. Other family members filled the cabin, and every available space was packed with a witch or a shifter.

"That's because I brought a truckload of honey baked goodies, and Elspeth supplied honey mead and witch shine for the drinkers. Currently, they're all having a beary ball." Lila giggled at her joke.

"Hey." Holly popped up next to her cousins. "I brought the games."

"I contend that drunk monopoly is an extinction level event." Lila poured a thick, creamy liquid into a blender, added pineapple chunks, and processed it until it was smooth. She poured the mixture into three glasses. "Bottoms up, ladies."

Holly grabbed the glass and sniffed suspiciously. "Can we trust one of your devilish concoctions? I don't need a dose of food poisoning."

Lila rolled her eyes. "It's my piña colada mocktail. Pineapple chunks and juice, coconut cream and ice, then blend. It's a Lila special." She gestured grandly.

Raising an eyebrow, Xandie sipped. Tart, cold, creamy goodness exploded in her mouth.

"Wow. Almost as good as chocolate milk on the rocks."

"Thank you. Thank you very much." Lila winked.

Xandie winced as a screeching, discordant noise behind them tore at her nerves like fingernails on a chalkboard. "Please don't tell me that's what I think it is?"

"I cannot tell a lie. Elspeth snuck it in." Lila topped up Xandie's glass. "Have another drink."

"I had one rule." Xandie slapped the kitchen bench. "Just one. And she still breaks it."

Holly nibbled on a nail. "Theo begged and Nash wanted to join in. The wicked witch caved."

Closing her eyes, Xandie took a deep breath in, then blew it out with deep, guttural groans. "I can do this. It's a few karaoke songs. Nothing big."

"Can you hear me, Point Muse?" Theo's voice purred over the microphone, filling every crevice of the noise-filled Lodge. "Let's rock it."

A roar gathered momentum around the room, and shifters and witches of all shapes and sizes leapt to their feet clapping. A catchy strain of a Gloria Gaynor song was overwhelmed by Theo's warbling.

"I will *not* survive. I must run away," Xandie moaned.

"Just wait. You haven't got to the light show yet."

"Hecate's tone-deaf eardrums. Can I leave yet?

"Look." Holly grabbed Xandie and spun her around on a chair.

Theo, Xandie's black cat, Colin, the mouthy pug, and Nash, Lila's hellhound, all stood on a makeshift stage. Theo paced front and center, caterwauling into a miniature microphone. Colin stood behind as a backup singer, and Nash let his hellhound eyes flame off and on, bright red lighting Theo in a hellish, pyrotechnic spotlight.

Xandie's aunt Amelia and uncle Shade giggled and cuddled on the couch, and Winifred and Elspeth cut a rug in front of the karaoke stage. Xandie closed her eyes to her grandmother's robotic twerking. Some things a granddaughter should never see.

"That's it. I'm tapping out for a breather." Xandie placed the glass on the bench and waved at her cousins before heading outside to the porch. She relaxed as the door shut behind her, enclosing her in relative peace.

"Quiet at last." Xandie leaned up against the porch rail and rubbed the back of her neck. The whole night, her skin had itched. If she hadn't had Lila look, she'd swear she had a rash, but nothing showed. Just a nebulous itch that she was beginning to think was an ominous feeling of impending doom. And knowing the Harrow bad luck, impending probably meant tonight. Maximum carnage, maximum mayhem should be a Harrow motto.

"But at least for the next few seconds, I have peace." Xandie closed her eyes, inhaling the dark scent of the forest that surrounded the lodge. The aroma of freshly churned earth and...*rotting meat?* Xandie opened her eyes and scanned the scene. Lights from the lodge lit a small area on the ground around the building. Everything seemed quiet and still, so where had that stench come from?

A skittering noise of claws on rocks came from one side, and Xandie turned to face it. The light from the lodge failed to penetrate the shadows, which seemed to thicken and congeal the longer she stared.

The door to the lodge burst open, and Holly stumbled out along with the earsplitting din of group karaoke. She cupped her hand over one eye. "I can't handle Elspeth twerking any longer. I swear I'm getting an eye tumor from the visual horror I just had to endure. The wicked witch is currently giving Braun's mother twerking lessons. It's a horror show. Don't look." Holly paused and eyed Xandie's unmoving form. "You okay there?"

"What do you see when you look at the corner of the lodge?"

"My cousin, who seems to be having some kind of mental crisis, and a lot of shadows." Another scuttling noise came from the other side of the lodge, accompanied by a large bang. Holly's eyes widened. "Are we about to be invaded? Did Theo's karaoke open a portal to the under-world?" Holly crowded in close to Xandie as a chittering noise sounded from the front of the lodge now. The girls angled to face the threat.

A surging carpet of black, shadowy bugs with gleaming, obsidian pincers flowed toward them.

Holly let out a piercing shriek and clutched at Xandie. "Where's an exterminator when you need one? Do you know the types of germs those things carried?"

"Can it, witches," Theo snapped as he marched onto the porch. "You're ruining my performance. I'm the only one who can carry off a note like that."

Claws scratching on wood sounded in the air as a demonic-looking black bug skittered toward Theo.

"Take the witches," the cat shrieked, frozen on the spot. "I can't die before my show at the wedding reception. It could be my big break." The rest of the surging crowd of insectoid killers raced toward the porch.

"Can't take you lot anywhere." Two hands yanked Xandie and Holly back inside, tumbling Theo along the floor until he lay inside the room. Elspeth slammed the door shut and locked it. "Cut the karaoke," she bellowed. "Make sure every door and window is locked down tight. We're under attack."

The music ground to a halt as everyone dashed forward, carrying out Elspeth's orders.

"Are you okay?" Zach stood next to Xandie and ran a hand up and down her arm.

She turned a wide-eyed gaze toward him. "Someone sent killer bugs to interrupt our party. I'm getting a complex."

"You'll survive." Elspeth snapped her fingers in front of Xandie's face. "Report. Now."

"I can." Holly jumped up and down with her hand in the air.

Sighing, Elspeth waved Holly on. "If you must."

"Pure, black, evil insects. Murderous pincers at the front and a thirst for human blood."

"For my blood," Theo cut in. "I barely escaped with my life."

Holly deflated. "I was going to say that next."

"Never mind, dear." Winifred patted her daughter on the back.

A screeching noise from one of the front windows drew everyone's attention.

"And their eyes are now going red like rabid vampires." Holly pointed at the window as tiny pinpricks of red appeared, pressed up against the glass, staring in at them.

Xandie threw her hands into the air. "Just perfect."

"Mutant-sized, broad-necked root borers." Winifred shrugged self-consciously as her family stared at her. "I like watching animal shows."

"They're called shiver bugs. We have them in the underworld for eating carrion." Shade, Lila's father, hand-in-hand with her mother Amelia, joined the group.

Lila looked at her father with a sick expression. "Do we want to know why they're called shiver bugs?"

"Because they prefer to eat live prey when they can get it. Their victims shiver and writhe in tortuous pain as the bugs feed. They prefer their prey...*alive*."

"Yep. Didn't want to know that."

"It's all right, baby. Daddy is here." Shade puffed out his chest and took a step forward, flexing his muscles. "I've notified Hades about what's happening. He should be here any second. He hates these bugs."

Colin poked his head out from underneath the food table. Partygoers had knocked plates of food to the ground in their rush to obey Elspeth. It was a veritable feast for the ever-hungry pug. Smeared remnants of something fishy covered his face. "Are the killer bugs gone yet? The drama's interrupting my digestive process."

Xandie shuddered and made sure her big, burly fiancé was between her and the pug. Colin's stomach digestive issues equaled a weapon of mass olfactory destruction.

"Did you just maneuver me into the line of fire?" Zach snickered and took a step to the side, exposing Xandie.

"We aren't married yet, and even if we were, I'm pretty sure our vows do not specify protection from radioactive stenches. You're fair game."

The sound of feet pounding along the upstairs landing drifted downstairs, followed by the mass exodus of the party guests down the stairs.

"We've got incoming," Melody bellowed as they joined the Harrows and the rest of the partygoers in the center of the room.

Glass tinkling and shattering upstairs fueled Elspeth, and she rolled the sleeves of her indigo-colored jogging suit up and cracked her knuckles. "Bring it on, bugs. It's exterminating time."

Xandie grabbed the karaoke microphone as a weapon. Everyone around her followed suit, including her fiancé, who grabbed a plate with a few remaining honey buns left on it. "Exactly how do you use honey buns as a weapon? Lila's cookies I can understand, but honey buns?"

"Hey," Lila protested with a weak grin. "Okay. My cookies are rock hard missiles, so I'll give you that one."

Zach grabbed the honey buns and stuffed them in his mouth, then brandished the plate like a bug-killing Frisbee. He chewed rapidly before swallowing and answering, "Like that."

"Needs must, I guess." Blowing out a breath, Xandie faced the ravening, black carpet that surged down the stairs. The room filled with enough chittering and skittering to satisfy the hardest of horror lovers.

Colin shot out from underneath the table and slapped multiple salmon pies on the ground before burying his face in them. Gobbling them down, he straightened and trotted past the group until he stood in front. His pudgy little body quivered as a green shade inched over his face and chest. "Yippee-kye-yay, evil bugs." Colin padded forward and turned his rump to face the beetle insurgents, just as Hades popped in with a blinding flash.

"Hades will save the day." With a snap of the god's fingers, the bugs exploded into obsidian-colored goo. A river flowed down the stairs, and puddles formed islands of black over the lodge floor. Hades smirked. "See? Nothing to be concerned about."

"Run," Xandie screamed and abandoned her microphone. She ran for the door, scrabbling to unlock it in time.

Zach pounded the floor behind her, panting down Xandie's neck. "Hurry, hurry," he chanted.

Hades frowned, confused. "The bugs are dead. There's no threat left."

"Incoming." A loud rumble erupted from the vicinity of the pug's tiny body, and he sank to the ground with a relieved expression.

Confusion vanished as horror dawned on Hades' face. The God of the Underworld let rip with a piercing shriek that shattered the remaining windows on the ground floor of the lodge. "Nooooo." The wailing God backpedaled away from the pug but slipped in a black goo puddle. Collapsing on his side, he lay full-length, flat upon the floor. Hades slowly blinked, focusing on the radioactive pug with a traumatized, glazed stare.

It's all about karma. No good deed should go unpunished. Especially when a seafood-challenged pug is in the room.

EIGHTEEN

"I think the third shower and a whole bottle of antibacterial body wash did the trick." Xandie sniffed at a lock of her hair.

"I'm not running the risk of repelling the customers." Lila patted the bright orange hairnet that covered her curly brown hair. "I'm hoping no see, no smell."

"Good luck on that." Holly slumped in a chair next to Xandie. "I'm betting the stench stays around for the rest of our short, olfactory-challenged lives." Then she pouted. "It's all right for the two of you. You both have significant others. I just have my spinsterhood."

Snickering, Lila deposited a plate of hot, savory muffins on the table. "I thought you wanted to run free, unencumbered by the ball and chain of a life partner."

Holly shrugged. "The solo life isn't all it's cut out to be."

Xandie checked out the bakery, devoid of customers or Harrows, except for her cousins. "Where is everyone this morning?"

"Elspeth picked up the wedding dress from the drycleaners and is upstairs in my apartment, making sure it's safe. Mom and Dad have headed down to the underworld to keep an eye on Hades. He's in therapy now and on stress leave. Apparently, the combination of lying in bug goo and Colin's stench is traumatic."

"He's not wrong." Holly shivered. "Even Mom slept with the light on last night."

"I just had to put up with Zach's whining about the loss of all the honey baked goods Lila had supplied for the party. So much whining, and don't get me started about Theo and his lost opportunity to practice karaoke. *I* need therapy." Xandie pouted. All joking aside, those skittering black bugs were nightmare-inducing.

"We're Harrows. We all need therapy." Holly frowned, her attention on the bakery window. "I think there's something wrong with Ruby." She pointed to the Devlin twin standing outside their shop, Sinful Desserts, hands to her mouth, shoulders shaking.

"Man. How about one day without drama?" Xandie dragged herself upright. "Right. Let's nip this drama in the bud and move onto the next wedding calamity."

The girls filed out of the bakery and stood there, staring at the woman on the other side of the road.

"Xandie," Ruby wailed as soon as she spotted the trio. She flapped her hands and rushed across the road without checking for traffic.

"Ruby. Stop," Lila yelled, but it was too late. As Dorothy and Olive's hairdressing van turned a corner, it nearly sideswiped the still crying Devlin twin.

The hairdresser wrenched the steering wheel and ran up onto the pavement outside the Devlins' dessert café, coming to a screeching halt. The back doors of the van sprang open, and boxes tumbled onto the ground, littering multicolored wigs across the road and pavement.

Lila and Holly rushed to Ruby, and Xandie raced to Dorothy.

Opening the driver's door, she leaned in. "Dorothy, are you okay? Did you hit your head?"

"I'm good, Xandie girl." She shook her lopsided lilac beehive-wig-wearing head. "I didn't see her. Maybe I need glasses for driving."

Xandie helped the older woman climb down from the driver's seat. "Ruby's upset for some reason and didn't look before crossing the road. It wasn't your fault."

"Ruby Devlin? Did I hit her? Is she okay?"

"Looks fine to me." Xandie rubbed the hairdresser's back.

Dorothy grabbed Xandie's hand tightly. "I just went out to pick up that rushed wig order for Elspeth." She dropped Xandie's hand, aghast. "The wigs." The hairdresser scuttled behind the van and moaned as she spied the wig spill.

"Nothing looks damaged. We just need to get them back into their boxes." Xandie winked. "The quicker we get them packed up, the less likely Elspeth is to have a wig-related meltdown." Between the two of them, they made quick work of the colorful mess.

Dorothy slammed the door of the van shut and whistled. "We're all done. I'll get the van around the back of the store, and hopefully no one will know." With a wave, she hopped back into the van and inched off the pavement.

Dusting her hands on her worn jeans, Xandie headed back to the still sobbing Ruby.

"You okay?"

"Xandie." Ruby launched herself at the Librarian. "I didn't see the van, but it missed me. I was too upset about your wedding cake."

Another issue. If she heard the *"w"* word mentioned

again, she'd scream. "What about my cake?" Xandie carefully pried the distraught woman off and handed her over to Lila.

Ruby gulped. "We had a surprise health inspection. They found your cake half eaten by mice. *Mice.* We've never had a mouse issue here ever."

"It's all right. Calm down. We'll sort this out."

"You don't understand. The inspector shut us down for code violations. We can't make your cake or any of the food for the wedding until they investigate and do more tests. I'm so sorry. We're letting you down."

"It's fine. It's all okay." Xandie bared her teeth in a grimace, then turned away and let loose a guttural scream.

"I love street performances." Hester, Lila's brownie employee, arched a graying eyebrow at the Librarian. "I take it the wedding planning isn't going well?"

"I. Don't. Want. To. Talk. About. It," Xandie gritted out.

"Right, on that discordant note, Hester and I will take Ruby back to her shop. You and Holly flip the bakery sign to closed and head upstairs and let Elspeth know what's happened." Lila directed Ruby back across the road. "I'm glad Nash is with Matthew at work and Colin's back at Harrow House. The last thing they need to see is Xandie losing her mind."

Hester shrugged and followed her boss. "The Harrows always make *me* scream."

Holly poked Xandie in the back as they entered the bakery and headed upstairs. "Maybe you should do primal therapy. It's screaming and stuff."

"I do feel better," Xandie admitted. "Who knew screaming your lungs out could feel so good?" She flung the door to Lila's apartment open and surprised Elspeth standing dead center in the apartment...*wearing the freshly dry-cleaned wedding dress.* "What are you doing?"

"Hecate's girded loins." Holly's eyes grew wider and wider.

"I had to see if it fit and if it was still comfortable." Elspeth and Holly's words collided into a shrieking ball of festering Harrow-caused headache. Xandie massaged her head as she stumbled farther into the apartment. She left the door open for a quick getaway after she slaughtered her grandmother.

Holly sidestepped away from Xandie and stood out in the open, hands in the air. "I, in no way, condone this wedding dress shenanigan and at the same time, still support and love both my cousin and grandmother." She partially lowered her hands. "Oh, and I'm not packing any type of projectile or hex-based weapon. Carry on."

"It's my dress. I'm just loaning it to you. Don't get so Meyers about it."

"*Now* you remember my last name?" Xandie narrowed her gaze on her grandmother. "And what do you mean by that?"

Elspeth sniffed and smoothed her hands down the sides of her cream-colored wedding dress. "You know. Like that father of yours. Persnickety and fastidious Meyers."

"You're wearing the dress I'm about to get married in—" Xandie raised her voice, but her words were cut off in a gurgle as someone ran into the room, slammed past her, and came to a sudden stop in front of Elspeth.

"Who'd have guessed the toad would turn up like a bad penny."

Edgar raised his head and stared at his wedding-dress-clad sister. He fought to speak through his shuddering breaths. Red patches painted his normally pale skin and sweat coated his face.

"Found out... Not. Not my fault. I... Coming..." He gasped, grabbing Elspeth's arm.

"He doesn't look so good, Elspeth." Holly drifted closer to Xandie. "In fact, does anyone know CPR? He looks like he might keel over with a heart attack."

Edgar did look exhausted and terrified. Not what you'd expected from a hardened killer and a nefarious wedding saboteur. Something was wrong. Grabbing Holly's arm, Xandie tried to drag her outside into the hallway, but it was too late. A stocky ninja-looking figure wearing a black mask bolted into the room and smashed an orange ball on the floor.

Smoke billowed out, shocking everyone out of their momentary paralysis from the masked ninja's entrance, but it was too late.

"Sleepy time hex," Elspeth had enough time to bellow before collapsing on the floor, her brother, Edgar, cocooned next to her.

"Hecate's blue balls," Xandie swore as she dropped, Holly a pace behind her. Xandie rolled over while she still could.

Without a care, and ignoring her helpless victims, the ninja made a phone call, whispering into the phone, "I didn't have a choice. I'll have to take them both. The Harrows can pay to have them both returned. I'll let you know when the deed's done. Everything's working out perfectly." The ninja let out a squeaky giggle, then resumed radio silence.

Elspeth had a last burst of energy and grabbed Edgar around the throat, trying to throttle him. "This. Is. All. Your. Fault," she whispered before collapsing.

The ninja giggled again, then grabbed an arm of each of the warring siblings and dragged them out of the apartment. After a few moments, the ninja popped back in and crouched beside Xandie, tapping her on the forehead. "Your wedding's dead in the water, Librarian. Deal with it." With that, the ninja disappeared, leaving behind that stinging zinger.

Xandie fought the lassitude floating over her. The need to scream at her family and the world drowned under the effects of the sleepy time hex. The one thing she knew was that pieces of the puzzle were finally falling into place. Because Xandie had heard the ninja's voice before. Recently... *Very recently*.

The game was afoot...

NINETEEN

"Who picked Elspeth kidnapped in a wedding dress?" Lila handed two bottles of water to her cousins.

Winifred held up a hand and waved wildly. "I did. I scooped the pool."

"You seriously picked Elspeth kidnapped in a wedding dress?" Xandie closed one eye as the late afternoon sunshine streamed into the Harrow House sitting room. "And also, how did I not know you were all betting on Elspeth getting kidnapped?"

Colin padded into the room and stopped next to Xandie's chair. "You Harrows. Someone was always gonna get kidnapped. Why not profit from it?"

"But in my wedding dress?" Xandie glared at the room. "*My* dress. Standing there in the middle of the room. *In my wedding dress.* Now it has Elspeth vibes."

"Technically, it *was* hers first. Which means her germs were on it before yours." Holly fake-gagged before guzzling more water.

"That's why I had it cleaned."

"And now it has extra Elspeth cooties and kidnapping vibes. Aren't you the lucky one." Lila poked out her tongue.

"How about we focus more on the kidnapping and less on the possible germs on the dress?"

"Speak the truth, Elspeth's wise granddaughter." Colin glared at the room. "I want my dame back. So, get on with the thing you Harrows do."

"You mean plan how we're going to get my wedding dress back?"

"And my grandfather." Liam leaned against the wall next to Xandie's mother.

The lights overhead pulsed for a moment as he spoke before settling down. The house was still excited about another Harrow. Every time Liam walked past or under a light, it flickered and popped, dimming and glowing with a cozy warm heat.

"And Edgar as well." Xandie started to nod but thought better of it. The sleepy time hex had worn off quickly after Liam and Lila had stormed her apartment. Thankfully, her Aunt Winifred had a dose of the antidote at her potions and candle store down the street. But it left a fierce headache and dry mouth behind.

Holly finished off her water. "Do we have any idea who the culprit is, or are we just waiting for a ransom?"

"On that cheery note, Aunt Winifred and I need to get cooking reception goodies. Let us know once you have a plan in place." Lila grabbed her aunt on the way out.

"What about my reward for picking a kidnapped Elspeth in a wedding dress?" Winifred grumbled as she left the room.

"Your family has an interesting way of coping with stress." Liam shifted and clasped his arms over his chest.

"Your family too. And we've been through this scenario before...unfortunately," Miranda admitted.

"You know we need a plan. Proof of life et cetera. I'm thinking the ransom note won't be far off." Dropping his arms, he paced up and down the length of the sitting room. "I can call in help, agents, black ops, other snipers. You name it. I have access."

Xandie's fiancé shifted on the couch. "Settle down, male Harrow. We've got plenty of experience, and Xandie knows what she's doing, most of the time." He rubbed her neck.

"Most of the time. *Ha ha.* So funny." Xandie elbowed Zach. She dropped the humor. "Edgar isn't the killer. He rushed into the apartment with something important to tell us earlier. He just didn't get a chance to tell us."

"He's an idiot but not a killer," Liam agreed.

Holly peered out the window. "Speaking of Edgar, has anyone informed Gigi yet?"

"No. I'll do that after this meeting."

"Sorry, Chief Braun. But you might need to speed up your timetable. She's outside."

Cursing, Xandie stood as an audible click sounded throughout the sentient house.

"I'm not up to deciphering Harrow House peculiarities today. Can anyone translate for a dense bear shifter?" Zach peered around the room, confused at the clicking noise.

"The house doesn't want non-family members inside with Elspeth gone. Harrow House is effectively on lock-down." Xandie headed for the front door and patted the wall next to it. "I promise I won't let anyone in, but you need to let me out, so I can break the news to her. She deserves that."

With a groan, the house swung the front door wide open.

Xandie blew the house a kiss and stepped onto the porch in time to see Gigi bend down and pick up a plain white envelope from the ground.

Edgar's fiancée held it out. "I think your mailman stopped short of the house today."

Hello, ransom demand. Xandie took the envelope and held it in her hands. "Can I help you, Gigi?"

The brassy redhead bit her shiny, glossed lips. "Have you seen my sweetie poo? I haven't seen him since this morning. He took off from the inn early, saying he had to speak to Elspeth. And I haven't seen him since."

"I can answer that." Zach stepped up next to Xandie. "I'm sorry to have to tell you this, but it seems from eyewitness accounts that Edgar has been kidnapped, along with his sister."

"What?" Gigi shrieked and slapped a hand over her mouth. Eyes wide with unshed tears, she held out a hand to Malcolm, Edgar's assistant. "I need tissues," Gigi sobbed. "Who could do this to my baby?"

"We're currently investigating, and I promise to update you if and when we receive any information about the situation."

Gigi used Malcolm's tissues to blot her eyes. "Thank you, Chief. I knew this would happen. Edgar's such a successful businessman. You hear stories about kidnappings and ransoms, but you never think it'll happen to you." She shredded the tissue in her hand. "I'll pay whatever the kidnappers want for both Edgar and Elspeth. I know he would never leave his sister in that situation by herself."

Xandie snorted. "With what money? Edgar's running on empty." From what Liam had said, bankruptcy was in her great uncle's immediate future.

"Excuse me?" Gigi reared back and ran into Malcolm. He steadied her for a few seconds before dropping his hands.

"Edgar's broke. That's why he's here in Point Muse, looking to squeeze Elspeth for cash."

"That's a lie." Gigi spat the words. "You have no clue what you're talking about. This is Elspeth polluting your thinking. You're just her mouthpiece."

"What don't we all calm down? I can follow Gigi and Malcolm back to the inn. Stay with them for a little while." Braun exchanged a glance with his fiancée as he stepped past. "I'll get you settled and make sure you're both safe before I leave."

"Safe," Gigi shrieked and turned, sobbing, to Malcolm. "I'll never be safe again until my sweetie's back home."

Malcolm patted his employer's back and rolled his eyes at Xandie. "Okay, Gigi. Let's get you back to your room. I'm sure this will resolve itself soon." He directed Gigi into the back of the car and slammed the door shut. "Sorry about that, Ms. Meyers. She gets excited and loves drama. If you have any updates about Edgar's status, please don't hesitate to reach out."

At least someone remained sane. Out of the two, she'd much rather deal with Malcolm than Edgar's fiancée. "We will. I'm sure the police chief will want to ask some questions about your late lawyer too." Might as well deal with two problems at once.

"Of course. We were shocked to hear about his death and the fact he wasn't actually a qualified lawyer." Malcolm shook his head. "That's why you never let Gigi deal with the hiring of employees." He slid into the driver's side of the car and pulled away.

"You believe her performance?" Zach stood on the porch, keys in hand.

"Let's just say one is more believable than the other." Xandie held up the envelope. "I'll let you know what the ransom note says."

"Be careful."

"Ditto, lawman." Xandie waited until her fiancé left. Then she opened the envelope and slid out a typed message. "Five hundred thousand for the two Harrows or they won't see the light of day. Time and place of exchange to be determined." That was it. Nothing else, and she'd be willing to bet if Braun checked the envelope and paper, it would be free of prints. "Time to update the rest of the clan." Xandie slid back inside and held the envelope up for all to see. "Five hundred grand in exchange for Edgar and Elspeth."

Miranda rubbed her hands. "About time the action started."

"Five hundred thousand?" Holly's voice cracked. "How are we going to raise that amount? Elspeth probably has a stash of cash, but she's not here. What do we do?"

"I need to make some phone calls." Liam disappeared into the hallway.

"Notepad and pen, now." Miranda pointed at Holly, who rushed out of the room before returning a few minutes later with the stationery supplies. "Right, we need to make sure everyone in the family's secure. Then we plan our rescue. I'm sure we'll get the place and time for the exchange at the last minute, so as to limit the amount of planning we can do."

Xandie held up her Elspeth-spelled mobile. "I need to let Felicity know what's going on. Make sure she's safe as well."

Miranda nodded as she and Holly crowded over the notebook, jotting down ideas.

Moving to the corner of the room, Xandie waited for Felicity to answer. The phone rang until an out of breath Felicity answered.

"Did I catch you at an awkward time?"

Felicity giggled nervously. "Hi, no, sorry, Xandie. I was just in the bathroom."

Felicity's voice cut in and out, and a rattling sound jangled in the background. "Sorry, Felicity. Reception isn't great. I need to let you know Edgar and Elspeth have been kidnapped. I wanted to make sure you're safe and secure."

"Oh, my goodness. That's horrible. Poor Elspeth and Edgar," Felicity said.

"If you're safe wherever you are, you need to hunker down. Stay put until I let you know it's okay."

"Yes, yes. Of course. I have no plans to go anywhere right now."

"Talk later." Xandie hung up and hid her phone away. "Mom? You need to raid Elspeth's creation cave for any sort of hex or spelled weapons you can get your hands on."

"You want to raid Elspeth's lair?" Holly opened and closed her mouth. "Are you sure that's the way to go? I mean, we don't even have a suspect like we normally do. Elspeth banked on Edgar, but it obviously isn't him."

"We have a suspect, and I know exactly where our family's being held."

"And I have the cash." Liam stepped into the room, still holding his phone. "The money will be here within the hour. But we can't rush this. We need a structured plan."

Xandie smiled slowly. "We have a plan. And for once, I'm taking a page out of the wicked witch's playbook.

Maximum carnage, maximum mayhem." It was time to rescue the warring Harrows and erase her wedding hex.

Time to take down their nefarious nemesis. They just had to survive Edgar and Elspeth fighting first.

Piece of cake for Point Muse's Sherlock Librarian.

TWENTY

"I hope you know what you're doing." Liam crouched next to Xandie behind a large bushy tree.

"Trust me. We have experience with takedowns. Not to mention, this isn't our first operation involving the church. We have prior knowledge of the interior." The church loomed like a dark blob in front of them, except for a warm glow of light from the windows that illuminated portions of the building and surrounding grounds.

"They aren't exactly trying to be covert. But kudos on using the empty church." Lila dragged Holly down next to her cousin. "What part of covert do you not get, banshee?"

"Hey. I get covert. I just didn't want to get muddy and catch a cold," Holly protested. "And it's empty because the rev refuses to step one foot inside the place until another exterminator has been through again. Once was obviously not enough."

"Rats gone," Nash growled. Flickering flames burst to life in his eyes for a few seconds before dying away.

Xandie scratched the hellhound behind his ears. "Yeah,

those rodents are long gone. Everyone know what you're doing?"

Holly cleared her throat. "I, for one, would like a final run-through." She smoothed her chin-length bob with a jerky hand. "Just in case."

"You'll be fine. Just follow me." Lila winked.

"I'm getting Xandie to repeat the plan *for you*. You never listen the first or second time," Holly sneered. "I don't want to get smacked by goo or any stray hex that paralyses me or turns me into a statue. So, listen up."

"Those instances are strangely specific. Should I be concerned?" Liam cocked his head. "Point Muse has a reputation amongst certain professionals. I thought a lot of it was rumor. Or overactive imaginations."

Lila snickered. "Holly's oddly specific because she's always in the wrong place at the wrong time. It's a talent. Probably her main Harrow talent, besides being a banshee." Lila frowned at her cousin. "Although lately, you haven't had any visions. Not even a twitch of your death talents. Are you on the fritz? It's not like we haven't had bodies around us."

"And it's not like I have an instruction manual on my banshee side. And I only speak to Dad every so often. Maybe I'm blocked." Holly poked a finger at Lila. "And I don't need any of Elspeth's prune juice either. It's not that kind of blocked. As for being specific, that's because I swear you and Elspeth aim for me."

"Maybe?"

"*Plan?* Does everyone remember the plan?" Xandie valiantly tried to drag her family back on track. "Mom's on the perimeter in case of a runner. Zach and his deputy are waiting just within the perimeter, with spotlights. They have orders to let people through the perimeter and once the situation is resolved take our killer into custody. Lila and Holly are going to lurk outside the church, entering when needed. Your job, Liam, is to get our kidnappees out safely. I'm inside with the money and distraction. Nash can work..." Xandie glanced around. "Nash has already gone?"

Lila shrugged. "He likes to do his own thing."

"As does Liam, it seems." Holly pointed at the now empty space Liam had occupied.

"As long as he doesn't get in our way, I don't care what he does." Liam might be a sneaky peaky clone of her mom, but the Harrows had experience with traps and rescues.

"I'm here with you, doll face. It's my dame in the poo-poo. I'll be there to save her. Count me in." Colin wrinkled his nose. "I've seafooded up, and I'm primed to fire. No leaving me behind."

As a threat, it was effective. No one wanted to risk olfactory putrefaction. "Keep out of the way and stay safe." She nodded at her family. "Let's do this." Xandie stood and adjusted her hold on a small gray backpack Liam had supplied with surprisingly real-looking fake cash. Striding toward the church, she paused on the front steps and took a steadying breath. No matter the mayhem she caused, Elspeth was her grandmother, and Xandie didn't want her hurt.

"You got this, girly. It ain't your first rodeo or ransom drop."

"Thanks, Colin." Now that she stood close to the church, low rumbles of voices drifted out to her.

"This is all your fault. If you hadn't come back, my granddaughter would be married by now."

"If you hadn't cheated me of my rightful inheritance, I wouldn't have had to come back to this witch town."

"Stop it. Stop it. Stop it," another person inside shrieked, then let out a nervous giggle.

"That's our cue." Xandie slammed open the door. The kidnapper spun, mouth open, and the warring siblings grew quiet for a moment, all staring at Xandie's entrance.

"*How*... We hadn't sent you the time or place of the ransom. How did you know where we were?"

"*Please*. I'm not that stupid. It wasn't hard to work out with all the background noise when I called. The church has a noisy generator. Or do you mean how did I work out the kidnapper was you...*Felicity?*" Xandie strolled into the church. All the benches had been helpfully pushed to the side, allowing for easy access. "Your squeaky giggle kind of gives you away. It's very distinctive. The ninja-dressed kidnapper giggled when they knocked out Holly and me and took Edgar and Elspeth." Xandie pointed to her family. "It wasn't hard to connect that giggle with the oh-so-helpful wedding assistant. Not to mention, you had the means and proximity to all the victims."

"You think you're so smart, but you don't know everything." Felicity smirked and held up a small rectangular box. "See this? Looks like a Taser, but it's been hexed up. I can take you all out with one push of the button. Just give me the money, and you Harrows can go free." She waved the Taser at Elspeth and her brother. "I'm sick of their squabbling anyway. I can't think when they open their gobs."

"You'd be amazed how often we hear that." Xandie spotted a low-to-the-ground shadow dart past, heading for the kitchen. *Colin on the prowl.*

"Don't you sass our kidnapper. Have some respect," Elspeth barked at her granddaughter. "Besides, what time is it? You should've rescued me hours ago. This incident might be the one to tip my sanity switch."

"One can only hope," Xandie muttered and then raised her voice. "You're lucky I'm rescuing you at all. You're wearing my wedding dress."

"She isn't wrong. Wearing the bride's dress is a huge no no." Felicity nodded, her nefarious goals forgotten for a moment.

"I should take the word of a killer and a kidnapper?" Elspeth blew a raspberry. "Not happening, psycho wedding killer."

"I. Am. Not. A. Killer," Felicity screeched. "Stop delaying and give me my money."

"I'm just waiting for the other rats to crawl out."

"Not a rat. How about a barracuda or an avenging angel?" Gigi strolled in through the church's open door, still dressed like Edgar's personal redheaded Barbie. "I'd say surprise, but you really aren't." As she strutted past Xandie, Gigi grabbed the gray backpack.

Xandie spun, but before she could do anything else, Gigi held up a crystal. "Now, now, Librarian. Don't be hasty. This is a psi bomb. If detonated, it will flatten the area and take out everyone's magical gifts. I suggest you back off."

"Gigi, how could you do this? I might squabble with Elspeth, but we're all Harrows. You're my fiancée."

Baring her teeth like a shark going in for the kill, Gigi took a few steps away from Xandie. "That's the point. I wanted the Harrows to suffer like I suffered. You're all murderers and must pay." Spit flew from Gigi's mouth as she paced and spewed her diatribe.

"Taken in by a pretty face, but not so pretty disposition.

Whack job isn't an attractive quality in my dating book. You're such a disappointment, Edgar."

"Shut it, Elspeth." Everyone in the room roared at the witch at the same time.

Elspeth subsided with a pout.

"Did I ever seem familiar to you?" Gigi trailed a finger down her cheek. "Mind you, I have had work done. Also, I changed my last name after my parents died. Charis had a little too much notoriety, but Charming was a perfect fit."

Edgar gasped "Charis was my first wife's last name."

"*Ding ding*. We have a winner." Gigi giggled. "Sylvie was my big sister. The only Charis worth anything. And the Harrows killed her."

"Didn't she die in childbirth?" Elspeth frowned.

"That doesn't make a difference. The Harrows took her town and family away. Her broken heart killed her."

"My parents knew the police were on their way to Harrow House to take Edgar in for a get rich scam. They told him to run, and he never looked back."

"Lies," Gigi fumed. "Edgar told them Sylvie was pregnant, and they didn't care. The Harrows kicked them out and sealed Sylvie's fate."

"Nope. The Charis family involved Edgar in their last scheme. Set him up as the fall guy. My parents gave him cash and told him to run. Said they'd sort everything out."

"*No.* Sylvie said they kicked them out. They had to run. She would have come back, but she didn't have the chance. And that's Edgar's fault. My parents told me everything. The Harrows gave evidence of the scam. The police had warrants, so my parents and I ran as well." Gigi sucked in a breath, her chest heaving. "Then they died in a car crash. I went into foster care, and I swore I would end the Harrows.

And look where we are now." She opened her arms wide, still holding onto the backpack with one hand.

Elspeth heaved a deep sigh. "At least tell her the truth, Edgar. Get it out in the open."

"You have to understand. I was a different man back then," Edgar pleaded. "Losing Sylvie woke me up. I had a baby, a son, dependent on me. I got into the ground floor of a vitamin business. It worked well for a long time."

Gigi dropped her arms and blinked glassy eyes. "What are you saying?"

"My parents gave me money, and they told us to run. They did give evidence of the scam to the police, but they didn't kick us out. Once we left, Sylvie didn't want to come back. She hated her parents scamming people."

"No. You lie."

"Sylvie planned to wait until you were a little older, and then she'd sweep in and grab you. Take you away." He ground to a halt. "But she died before she could."

"I don't care what you say. Even if you weren't kicked out, you still took her away and killed her." Gigi shook the red crystal at her fiancé. "And you're all going to pay."

Xandie reached into her pocket and held out a handful of rainbow-colored balls. "I have my own ammunition." She'd deal with the Elspeth creation cave fallout later. For now, it was time for Xandie to foil the nefarious nemesis, destroy her wedding jinx, and save the day.

And better yet...Elspeth will owe me.

TWENTY-ONE

"Why you little Librarian snake. Those are mine, from my creation cave." Elspeth wiggled wildly before resting with a curse. "You're all gonna pay big time for your invasion of my privacy. Underwear drawers cursed shut for the whole family for six months. Revenge is mine."

"Stuff it, Harrow. This is my rescue plan. Next time, we'll do it your way... If we survive this." Xandie raised her hand and threw the balls to the ground. They exploded with a hiss and a pop. Rainbow smoke gathered in a thick rolling cloud that quickly spread along the ground. The level rose to Xandie's knees in the blink of an eye.

Colin scooted out from the kitchen and waited at the side exit as Lila and Holly bolted in from the other side and grabbed hold of Gigi. Holly snatched the crystal out of her hand and held it up like a trophy while Lila grappled with the stiletto-clad Barbie killer.

Felicity opened and closed her mouth like a fish gulping its dying breath. "This wasn't the plan." She held out her trembling Taser. "Stop it, or I'll shoot you all."

"That would be a feat, considering they gave you a dud."

"Dud?"

Xandie nodded. "It's a fake."

"No. I tried it on Edgar. It works."

"Only enough charge for a couple of shots. You were set up as the fall girl. The dupe and the mother, all trussed up for the cops."

"You are definitely the smartest Harrow." Malcolm strolled out from behind the altar at the front of the church. "Maybe too smart for your own good."

"Maybe. Smarter than your minions, though. When did you decide to double-cross your lover and your mother?"

"What?" Felicity shrieked. "He'd never double-cross me. He loves me."

"And I'm his mother. We're blood. He'd never dare," Gigi hissed.

Malcolm stepped in front of the exit door, with a no-nonsense, dark gray pistol in hand. "You're all getting what you deserve. Mom has always been obsessed with the Harrows. Then she concocted this whacked-out plan when she heard about the wedding. It wasn't hard to find someone on the inside." He nodded at Felicity. "She was easy to fool with a fake love affair. And poor little Gigi never saw the double-cross coming." He waggled his gun. "Throw the bag over here, dearest mother, or I'll shoot you through your thick skull."

Gigi punted the bag at her son. "You little worm. Double-crossing me. *Me.* Of all people," she spluttered, fists clenched.

"You're the one who taught me the art of the grift and looking after yourself. You shouldn't be so surprised."

"You never loved me?" Felicity sagged, still holding onto her now useless Taser.

"All part of the con, sweetie." Malcolm winked. "You should be proud you did such a good job. No one suspected anything except for the smarty-pants Librarian."

"Man. I need some popcorn. Live theatre is a blast," Elspeth announced.

Inclining her head slightly at Holly, Xandie stepped a little closer.

Holly sidled over to stand next to Elspeth and Edgar, surreptitiously working on their bound hands.

"He's the killer, not me," Gigi screamed and launched herself at her son, taking a surprised Felicity with her at the same time.

Malcolm stepped back and ran into the muscular chest of Liam Harrow.

"I have a bone to pick with you." Liam grabbed Malcolm's gun and dropped it to the ground, kicking it past the frantically screaming Gigi.

Still holding tight to the backpack, Malcolm swung it at Liam and managed to shake himself from the male Harrow's grip. Standing with the open exit door and Colin behind him, Malcolm reared back, preparing to let loose with the bag again.

Anticipating this move, Liam let fly with a lightning quick punch to the nose.

Malcolm groaned, holding his nose with one hand. He stumbled back, failing to see a waiting Colin who reared up and nipped at the killer's ankle. Shrieking, Malcolm's arms windmilled as he flew through the air, hitting the ground just outside the exit door, the bag of fake cash still along for the ride.

"You mess with one Harrow, you mess with them all."

Colin padded outside to the villain, who was groaning on the ground, still flat on his face. "Crime never pays, fathead." The pug climbed on top of Malcolm's back and jiggled around for a moment.

Holly released the siblings, and everyone, including Gigi and Felicity, crowded the doorway as the police spotlighted the moaning Malcolm and the victorious pug.

"Why's Colin twerking like that?" Holly grimaced. "Maybe he shouldn't hang out with Elspeth as much. His version of Elspeth's victory twerk needs work, and it's not a good look for a talking pug anyway."

Xandie's eyes widened. "That's not a victory twerk," she roared. "Fire in the hole."

Lila and Holly reacted with lightning reflexes and shoved Gigi and Felicity out the door to join Malcolm.

Xandie slammed the door shut behind them, just in time as a wave of green flowed from Colin's toes to his muzzle. With one final wiggle, he relaxed and sagged on the back of his victim.

A high-pitched wailing and the sound of uncontrollable vomiting filled the air.

Backing away from the door, Xandie placed an arm over her mouth just in case.

Colin, Elspeth's weapon of mass olfactory destruction, was always an effective last resort.

The pug's bowel habits take no prisoners...

TWENTY-TWO

Baby pink roses formed a canopy over the nine Muse statues that surrounded the about-to-be-wedded couple.

The Library had outdone itself. Rosebushes bloomed in a carpet of deep rich red flowers interspersed with the lush, green grass of the back yard. White wooden chairs lined the rose-petal-covered aisle. Farther back, tables and chairs ringed a marble dance floor.

"I ain't up here by myself. Pay attention." Elspeth rattled the open book in her hand to get Xandie's attention.

The wicked witch had dry-cleaned her wedding dress again and opted to wear it to the wedding with matching combat boots and flowing, silver-blonde, be-wigged locks. Thankfully, Xandie's father had saved her wedding by supplying a beautiful ivory, Grecian style wedding gown, knotted at one shoulder, with matching pastel bridesmaids' dresses. Dorothy and Olive had tamed Xandie's unruly hair and piled it into a mass of curls on top of her head, secured with a crown made of flowers supplied by the Library.

"Well, Librarian?" Elspeth glared. "Don't make me look bad up here."

"You looking bad has nothing to do with me. Carry on with the marrying." Xandie grasped Zach's sweaty hands tight. Her handsome bear shifter had cut his shaggy hair again and had donned an elegant, dove gray suit. Her father, proud of the groom's sartorial elegance, had declared the police chief matched his beautiful daughter.

"Right then. Let's move on." Elspeth opened the book, intoning. "Does anyone choose to object? And be aware, if you do, the wrath of the wicked witch of Point Muse will come for you." She pinned the crowd with a narrowed stare. "No takers?" She nodded. "Good listening skills. Xandie Meyers, are you marrying this disreputable shifter?"

Only Elspeth could call a police chief disreputable. Xandie looked over the crowd. Friends and family filled the chairs to overflowing. Even the Penne dragons, including her friend and dragon slayer Priss, had turned out in force.

Priss angled her head at Liam Harrow, wearing a carbon copy of the groomsmen's gray suits. She slowly winked and fanned herself.

Holding back a smirk, Xandie turned to face her groom. There might be another Harrow romance on the horizon. Holly needed to pick up her dating game.

Zach tightened his grip on Xandie's hands. "If you want to run, I can tackle Elspeth and hold her down. That way, you can get away as quickly as you can before she blows."

Leaning in, Xandie whispered, "Do you really want to be seen wrestling your grandmother-in-law at a wedding altar while she's wearing a wedding dress?"

Braun paled. "Not quite the wedding I'd imagined, but I'd do it for you."

She snickered. "Yes. I want to marry you, Zachary Braun. That's if you think you can cope with all the future mayhem."

"I've been handling your family's dramatics for years. I've got Harrow wrangling experience."

Xandie leaned in and pressed a sweet kiss across his lips. "Meyers, not Harrow."

"No...Braun, not Harrow or Meyers." He swept in and draped her over his arms, kissing her deeply.

Elspeth threw her book over her shoulder. "Guess we don't need that now. You derailed my service, and I went to all that trouble getting ordained on the tree of life website."

"Don't worry," Zach whispered to his wife. "I booked us a civil service in Portland in case her service wasn't legal. You aren't getting away from the long, furry arm of law enforcement this time."

"For once, I'm happy for the fuzz to catch me."

Poking a finger down her throat, Elspeth pretended to vomit into a rosebush.

"Welcome to the chaos." Xandie winked.

***

"It's a fair offer. Think it over, Liam. You'd join the force as my deputy and take over Lila's boyfriend's empty apartment. He doesn't need it since he's moved in with her. With so many Harrows in town, I need all the expert help I can get."

Xandie snickered from her perch, tucked into her new husband's side. Edgar had moved into Harrow House, and the siblings lived to argue with each other. They were both having the time of their lives. With Liam's help, her husband could get a handle on any sort of mayhem and chaos the brother and sister caused.

"I'll accept your offer. I think I'm uniquely qualified to help you babysit Harrows."

A sharp gasp froze Liam as his grandfather slunk up next to him.

"Say it ain't so. Betraying your family name." Edgar blinked blearily at his grandson.

Elspeth took a swig from her hip flask. "No Harrow has ever gone to the dark side. Law enforcement." She shook her head in disgust. "Black ops and underhanded spy business, fine, but law enforcement? It just isn't done." Elspeth offered her flask to Edgar, who took a bracing, healthy gulp.

Months ago, Elspeth's hip flask had disappeared. Now it looked like her grandmother had resurrected it in honor of the occasion. *And she's sharing...* Xandie called this personal growth.

"Such a disappointment." Edgar took another swig and followed Elspeth as they headed to a far corner, heads together, whispering.

As one, Liam, Zach, and Xandie shuddered at the image.

"You know what? Maybe you should get Liam's signature on a work contract before those two come up with a scam to stop him from working for you."

"Good point." Zach grabbed Liam and headed toward the Library without a backward glance.

"Such is the power of Elspeth Harrow," Xandie intoned, and then giggled to herself.

A rosy, pink glow spread across the outside of the Library like a romantic light show. The Library had outdone itself for the wedding. It approved of her new husband and thrived on the energy that now filled the building. It was happy, and so was Xandie.

She faced the crowd of partygoers and let her gaze drift over the group. Her mother and father danced slowly to the magical assassin's cello rendition of AC/DC tunes. Lila and

Holly, along with Lila's boyfriend Matthew, wiggled on the dance floor.

Nash and Colin lay under the food table, licking icing from their faces. The hellhound nibbled on the flowers braided into his collar.

Xandie lifted her face to the late afternoon sun and inhaled. Warmth spread over her skin, and the scent from the roses blooming around her cocooned her in happiness. This was always where she was supposed to end up. The person she was meant to be.

She'd found her place.

Xandie's spiritual ruminations ground to a halt as a discordant, sharp note sounded and AC/DC ground to a halt. And instead, a different tune took its place. Xandie backed up a step, shaking her head. "No. Not that song. Never that song. I left instructions for it to never be that song."

"This is dedicated to the bride and groom. May their love go on and on," Theo yelled into the microphone, held by Dorothy, the hairdresser.

The magical assassin cellist winced but bravely accompanied Theo's powerhouse ballad.

Xandie's enjoyment of the wedding reception was going down just like the Titanic. She picked up the skirt of her wedding dress and bolted for the Library.

Some things a Harrow-Meyers-Braun just couldn't stick around for.

"My heart will go on and..."

The end.

Want More?
You can sign up for my mailing list. It's for new releases and no spam. Be the first to grab specials, new releases, and freebies.

Sign up now

https://www.kellyethan.com/newsletter

LEAVE A REVIEW

Did you like this book?

Please leave a review for it on Amazon!

The Nefarious Nemesis and the Wedding Jinx

ABOUT THE AUTHOR

I want to thank everyone who spent the time to read my novel.

My world is small town magic, mystery and mayhem, with plenty of snarky laughs along the way.

With an overactive imagination and a love of all things that go bump in the night, it was natural to write cozy paranormal mysteries, but I also love paranormal romance. No matter the genre, I love sarcastic heroines who like to save the day and solve the puzzle.

With a busy and chaotic household, writing is my outlet for madness. I live in Australia and when not writing, I can be found plotting my next fictional murder or chasing after the family's ferocious hellhound.

Visit me today at my website or say hello on social media.

Website:
https://www.kellyethan.com

COZY PARANORMAL MYSTERY:

Point Muse Cozy Paranormal Mystery Series

The Wicked Witch and the Christmas Chaos
The Wicked Witch and the Stolen Snow Globe
The Conniving Carver and the Jeering Jack-O-Lantern
The Wicked Witch and the Ultimate Smackdown
The Wicked Witch and the Abominable Snowman
The Wicked Witch and the Killer Grinch

#0 The Pernicious Pixie and the Choked Word
#1 The Killer Knight and the Murderous Chairleg
#2 The Dastardly Dragon Killer and the Poisoned Breath
#3 The Murderous Monster and the Stony Gaze
#4 The Cursed Crow and the Deadly Hex
#5 The Slanderous Siren and the Grievous Gift
#6 The Vengeful Villain and the Cursed Treasure
#7 The Fiendish Foe and the Deadly Jewels
#8 The Nefarious Nemesis and the Wedding Jinx

Point Muse Cozy Paranormal Mystery Boxed Set: Books 1-3
Point Muse Cozy Paranormal Mystery Boxed Set: Books 4-6
Point Muse Cozy paranormal Mystery Boxed Set: Books 1-8

LILA HARROW: Point Muse Cozy Paranormal Mystery

Cookies, Curses and Christmas Corpses.
#1 Cupcakes, Corpses and Chaos
#2 Pies, Potions and Peril
#3 Sin, Sugar and Shadows
LILA HARROW Point Muse Boxed Set: Books 1-3

HOLLY HARROW: Point Muse Cozy Paranormal Mystery

Banshee, Vikings and Voodoo
#1 Banshee, Death and Disarray
#2 Banshee, Moonshine and Madness
#3 Banshee, Sea Monster and Sabotage
HOLLY HARROW Point Muse Boxed Set: Books 1-3

The Ghost Vein Mine Cozy Paranormal Mysteries

#1 Ghosts and Gold Dust
#2 Curses and Cold Cases

Non Fiction

Heart and Craft.